RH
RIVERHOUSE
PUBLISHING

SOME MEN NEVER FORGET...

Vasily's Revenge:

The Complete Story

The Medlov Men Series

Latrivia S. Nelson

Vasily's Revenge: The Complete Story

The Medlov Men Series

Latrivia S. Nelson

Vasily's Revenge
RiverHouse Publishing, LLC
1509 Madison Avenue
Memphis, TN 38104

All **RiverHouse, LLC** Titles, Imprints and Distributed Lines are available at special quantity discounts for bulk purchases for sales promotions, premiums, fund-raising and educational or institutional use.

First RiverHouse, LLC Trade E-Book Printing 9-30-2014

Report abuse to the FBI at www.fbi.gov.

www.latrivianelson.info

www.riverhousepublishingllc.com

This book is dedicated to the lovely women of the Latrivia Nelson Love Pub on Facebook and the Medlovians across the world.

I love all of you.

Acknowledgments

This book would not have been possible without the love and support of my family and friends. To my children, thank you for giving me a higher purpose in this world. To my fiancé Bruce Welch, thank you for the words of encouragement and sometimes *just the words*. To my editor and co-captain, Karen Moss, who has listened to me whine, complain, cry tears of joy and even accepted my drunk calls, thank you for seeing the vision in my work. To my mentor, Deidre Malone, thank you for pushing me to push myself to the limit, knowing that it would take just that to succeed. To my fabulous diva beta readers: Leonie Radway, Natasha Kelly and Michelle Jackson, thank you for your sleepless nights and candid feedback. To my awesome moderators of the Love Pub Ernestine C-Riley, Andrea Degenett, and Cassandra Rios, and to all my fans who have stuck with me through thick and thin. Each and every one of you has been a blessing in my life.

Prologue

Manhattan, NYC
10 years ago

Even from downstairs in the Upper East Side three-story, luxury brownstone, Vasily could hear Lilly and his boss Leo arguing. The sound of raised voices and heavy objects hitting the wall and breaking were like nails on a chalkboard for him, reminding him of his less-than-fortunate childhood and the grizzly scenes that had unfolded at his father's hand.

After so many years of being around constant and abhorrent violence from a toddler to a grown man, he knew trouble brewing when he heard it. He also knew when a man was headed toward a vehement eruption, and based upon the growl in his boss's voice and aggressive words coming from his mouth, Lilly would be in trouble soon, if they both didn't calm down.

Lilly was a voluptuous woman, the kind who looked like she was born to be a centerfold pinup. With a large, double-D bosom, a freakishly small waist and wide sculpted hips, she had captured everyone's attention in the house, including

Vasily's but he never let on about it.

There was something charming about her raspy, seductive voice and smooth coco skin; the way her lips curved into a heart and her almond-shaped, brown eyes always showed all of her emotions. Her hair was like soft black feathers and the dimples in the sides of both of her high-cheeks seem to explode every time that she smiled at him.

And Lilly smiled often, despite his attempt to be as dull and quiet as possible around her.

In fact, he often avoided her just so that he wouldn't have to take in her intoxicating scent or try to hide the primitive reaction she caused in him.

Fresh out of hair school and going nowhere fast, she had fallen into Leo's arms at an upscale night club in Manhattan where she was a waitress. His romance of her was quick and to the point. He wanted her. So, he took her.

In exchange, she got this...

It was a lesson in the fact that all that glitters is not gold.

Looking up at the crown molding ceiling of the parlor Vasily shook his head at the vibrations coming from above.

They were not calming down. If anything, they were ramping up.

Another vase slammed against the wall upstairs, this time knocking down a painting with it. The clanging of the objects was only magnified by the constant name calling, not by her but by him. Leo berated her loudly, using his tongue instead of his hand for the moment to tear her down layer by layer.

There was only so much of this that Vasily could take, but the men sitting around the table with him seemed to be able to ignore it as they cleaned their guns, loaded their magazines and watched television like nothing was going on.

Some of them even ate their dinner and had sidebar conversations, never flinching as a woman just up the stairs screamed to the top of her lungs. To them, such a thing was typical, if not expected. Many of them had come from homes just like his, but had no better ideas of women than the men who had beat them and their mothers.

Vasily, on the other hand, swore to never hit a woman and never to allow one to be hit in his presence. Sure, there were evil women, no different from evil men in the world. But if he had to kill one, he did just that—respectfully with a bullet.

Taking a deep breath, he set down his Uzi on the round wooden table care-fully and stood up, pushing his chair a few feet away in frustration.

Most of the men sitting around the table did not paid attention to him. They could not possibly fathom that he was actually about to do something as stupid as intervene between their boss and his girl. Besides, they were supposed to be getting ready for a meeting tonight where money and microchips would be exchanged at an undisclosed location, not dealing in things domestic.

"Don't do it," Yakov warned his friend in a thick Russian accent. He sat beside him at the table, watching Vasily's demeanor change with each and every scream. "It's not worth it." He looked up at Vasily with old wisdom in his young features and shook his head, begging him to mind his own business.

Yakov had been with Leo longer than Vasily and knew his boss's hellish tem-per and his history with women. What was going on up-stairs was nothing new for the house. There had been many women before Lilly and would probably be many after her.

A hiss escaped him in anger. "I can't just sit down here and listen to this," Vasily said, clenching his square jaw. He looked up at the ceiling again impatiently. "He could be hurting her this time. Every argument gets one step closer."

"They are just arguing. No big deal. Tomorrow they'll be better," Yakov promised. "Besides, she's not your girlfriend. But he is your boss. Remember that." He pointed at him to add levity to the situation. "Don't do anything stupid."

Lilly yelled again, this time louder. The door to their bedroom flung open. "Fuck you, Leo!" she screamed. "I am so sick of dealing with your shit! You are not my father!"

"Get your black ass back here," Leo ordered in a thick Russian accent, bolting out of the door after her with his black Armani shirt open to show his sinewy muscles and a tattooed chest.

Grabbing her by her slender arm, he swung her around and slapped her across the face all in one motion.

Instantly, she fell to the carpeted floor, grabbing her face and crying. She was stunned that he had actually hit her this time. With wide eyes of disbelief, she looked up at him deathly afraid.

The hit echoed as the men went silent in the room below.

His heart strained. "That's it," Vasily said, voice going sharp as he headed through the doorway.

"Vasily, no!"

Yakov was immediately torn. Vasily was his best friend and like a brother to him, but Leo was his boss and he was his second-in-charge. He knew that Vasily wasn't wrong for wanting the fighting to stop. Lilly, after all, was a good and decent girl, but it was not their place to save her from a situation that she had put herself in.

Yakov stood up to go after Vasily, but gave him a moderate and intentional start. This was going to happen at one point or another. It might as well happen while he could help Vasily. He knew, while never saying a word, that Vasily had a thing for Lilly, but he also knew that his friend had never made one advance toward her. Vasily wasn't like that. He was more honorable than any other man that he knew in the Vory v Zakone. And it would be his honor that would be his ultimate downfall.

"What do you want us to do?" one of the other men asked, not really alarmed by Vasily's outburst.

Yakov motioned for the men to stay seated. "I've got this," he said, refusing to put his friend into danger without cause.

Everyone sitting at the table was the shoot now, ask questions later type. Even if they had to kill Vasily, they wouldn't care. He was one of them, but not really. He was newest to their small crew and only close to Yakov.

Headed up the elaborate alabaster wood staircase toward Lilly's cries, Vasily saw Leo look over the banister at him. He rushed as fast as he could, moving up the stairs two or three at a time, seeing red, determined to make the man stop his shouting and hitting.

As Vasily arrived on the third floor, heaving furious breaths, Leo scowled at him. His penetrating gray eyes were like a wolf locked on his prey. "What the fuck do you think you're doing?" he asked in a deep baritone, still standing over Lilly like he was ready to attack again.

He looked down at the woman, wearing only a torn pink satin slip, lip bleeding and long black hair covering her bruised face. Unable to help himself, Vasily reached out for her. All he wanted to do was to protect and keep her safe, only he didn't know why. "Get up," he said to her with both authority and concern.

Leo snorted in response. "Are you serious?" He frowned; looking around like someone was playing a practical joke on him. "What is this?"

"She's had enough," Vasily snarled. "I'm not disillusioned by what kind of men we are, but we don't beat women."

Leo's mouth dropped open when he realized that Vasily was serious. "I do whatever the fuck I want to do," Leo reminded, hitting his chest like a caveman. He stood between Vasily and Lilly, purposefully guarding his territory.

Leo was a big man, not easily pushed around or intimidated. Nearly as wide as Vasily, he boasted a thick, muscular chest and bulging arms and bottomed out with legs as large as tree trunks that were covered in tailored black slacks and leather dress shoes. His low black crew cut outlined his chiseled features—gray eyes, wide-lips, tanned skin, thick black brows and a splash of freckles across his face. He was menacingly handsome and overtly dangerous.

Leo gestured at the quivering woman while keeping his eyes on Vasily. "You're fucking her, aren't' you?" He wiped his nose and planted his feet ready for a fight.

Vasily stepped closer. "No." His tone was bitter and unapologetic. "If I were, I would not have let you lay the first hand on her."

Lilly pushed to her feet, forgetting the pain in her face for a second. She wiped her bloody mouth. "Leo, don't. Let's just go back inside and talk this out. There is no need to get any-one else involved." Her voice nearly failed her. She didn't want anything to happen to Vasily because of her. She liked him, more than he knew.

Leo laughed. "Oh, this is rich. You and my fucking foot boy? Really?" He looked between the both of them and put his hand on his hip in contemplation.

"Vasily has never touched me," Lilly answered.

"I just don't like men beating women," Vasily said, eyes narrowing. "I don't care who you are. I'm not going to let you put your hands on her again."

"Is that a fact?" Leo's fangs began to show. He was amused somewhat by the ridiculous attempt.

Yakov came up the stairs behind them, assessing the situation quietly. He looked over at Leo with faux-confusion. "What's going on?" he asked, although he already knew.

"Are you fucking her too?" Leo asked Yakov.

"No, Boss." The look on Yakov's face, a mix of surprise and denial, made Leo turn his attention back to the six-foot-four wall of muscle that was Vasily.

"Let me explain something to you," Leo said walking over to Lilly and grabbing her up by her neck. "This is my property." He pointed at Vasily. "You are my property, and if I choose to beat her or you then it's my fucking business. Until you are boss, you don't have a thing to say about it. Do I make myself clear?"

Vasily could feel the heat growing under his collar. "Let go of her," he demanded. "I won't say it again."

Lilly's brown eyes were filled with shame and fear. "Stop, Leo, please!" she begged.

Leo rubbed his jaw in contemplation. "Let go of her?" he asked, pushing her body against the banister as if he would push her over. "Here?" He pushed her harder and she screamed. "Or here?" He almost smiled at the reaction on Vasi-ly's face.

As half of Lilly's body dangled over the edge of the railing, Vasily went for the gun in his holster at lightning fast speed.

Pointing it at Leo's head with his finger on the trigger, he heard the distinctive click of a weapon behind him.

"Don't do this," Yakov begged, gun pointed. His friend had pushed his hand, leaving him no choice but to protect his boss.

"You throw her over, I pull this trigger and Yakov pulls his. Three people die. Won't be the first three; won't be the last. It's that simple," Vasily said without blinking. His greenish-blue eyes were intense under dark lashes and arched brows. "I really don't give a fuck if I live or die as long as I take you with me. But one thing is for sure, if you push her over that railing, you're next."

Lilly screamed, crying for her life and looking down three floors at the daunting marble floor beneath. Her two-carat diamond necklace broke and fell below as Leo squeezed her neck. There was no doubt that if he pushed her over, she would fall to her death.

Pushing her hands against the railing to keep from going over, she struggled. "Please, Leo. Don't do this? I'm sorry. God, I'm sorry, just please let me go!"

Vasily gripped the gun tighter, a bead of sweat forming at his left temple. "I'm waiting," he bit out.

Leo calculated the impending risk. In all the time that he had had Vasily un-der his employ, he'd never known him to bluff. This was not an idle threat, nor was it a good situation for him.

Yakov's hand shook, not because he was afraid to kill, but because he didn't want to kill the person in front of him. "Vasily, think of what you're doing," he said in a calm voice.

"I am thinking," Vasily said, not taking his eyes off of Leo.

Leo wasn't exactly anxious to end his life over a woman that he'd only met the year before. And there was no way that he wanted to be shot by one of his own men. There was no honorable death in that. He'd be the laughing stock of the Vory v Zakone in New York.

Snatching her back over the banister, he threw her on the floor against the wall.

Vasily looked down at her and reached for her again. "Come with me," he said softly. "Don't stay here and put up with this shit."

Lilly looked at his hand and started to cry. She wanted to leave more than anything, but she was afraid. Where would they go? Where would they hide from a man like Leo Rasputin? He was everywhere and knew everyone. He would find them and kill them.

Vasily's face was awash with disappointment and rejection as he watched her recoil away from him.

Leo laughed, already acutely aware of the outcome. "You see, you're the only one here who doesn't know his place." He put his index finger over his lips as he gave a crooked smile. "But let me remind you."

Suddenly, a gun went off behind him as a man, who had gone unseen the entire confrontation, standing in a few feet back from the four of them in the hallway released a round that went straight through Vasily's back.

It seemed as though time slowed down.

As the bullet exited his chest, Vasily dropped to his knees and looked across at Lilly one last time. Falling forward on the carpet, blood splattering out of his mouth, he finally released his gun.

As Vasily wheezed a gurgling violent last breath, Leo spit on his open wound and kicked the gun across the floor. "Get this piece of shit out of here," he said, stepping over him.

Even as the light faded from Vasily's eyes, he could hear Lilly's screams. She cried as Leo drug her down the stairs out of the view of the man who had tried and failed to protect her.

Chapter 1

Under a picturesque evening sky of the sun preparing for a triumphant setting on the now bluish, gold horizon, a small group of brooding men were released from the strong holds of their ironclad cells into the patchy, muddied, over-run recreational grounds of the Attica maximum security correctional facility for their daily one-hour walk in the yard.

With armed guards up on the risers holding binoculars, serrated barbwire covering the tops of the mountainous white-washed walls and additional men walking the perimeter with weapons and radios, there was not an ounce of freedom or opportunity in the fresh air.

Still the group of prisoners walked in the yard, huddled together, taking in the macabre view and laughing quietly like it was another carefree day at the beach.

Despite the system's best efforts, not much could affect Leo Rasputin or the men of the Rasputin Organized Crime Family. None of the men of the family were related, but they were in all ways relatives. They trusted no one who did not wear their tattoos or did not do crime with them. They only held sacred the laws of their governing body, the Vory v Zakone, and despite the warden's efforts to break them, they feared no man, recognized no government and took no prisoners.

In fact, it was their basic tenants on life that had kept them secluded from other prisoners for quite some time.

Nearly six months ago, a bloody, murderous riot in the mess hall started by another prison gang and aimed at the assassination of the Rasputin leader, Leo, had left them with no choice but to revert back to the savage creatures that they were. Never had such carnage been recorded within the walls of Attica since the riot of 1971, an event that made history and set new rules for prisons across the country. After that, the Rasputin men became historic figures in their own right. No more was there a question of who was the deadliest gang on the yard.

The warden, a simple man with Christian values and small stature, had developed a plan after that to get Leo under control. Only nothing about the plan had worked. Confining him to solitary did nothing. Taking away his privileges and visitors did nothing.

And threatening Leo had done only one thing. Piss him off.

Most of the guards were too scared to be truly aggressive, and none of the other prisoners would dare go near them.

Very recently, pissing Leo off had led to a strange order of events, including the warden's 21-year old daughter being in a near life-threatening car wreck, his home being set on fire in the middle of the night and his grandmother, who was in a retirement home in Montana, being found in Las Vegas four days later in a hotel tied to a bed with a note that simply said '*Checkmate*.' And all of the events happened within one week of the warden simply ordering that Leo be *roughed up*.

Now, there was only the final solution left.

There were no more answers for the new warden, who had only recently taken over after the death of the hard nose warden before him, who had in fact taken over after the 1971 riots. There was no proof that Leo was responsible for what had happened outside of the prison walls to his family, no end in sight to what could happen and no time for a transfer. The warden had to handle things now.

Staring out of his window through elegant drapes, dark wooden blinds and bullet proof glass, Warden C. W. Stowe sipped on his gourmet green tea, watched the men whom he loathed more than Satan himself walk the grounds, and waited patiently as Frédéric Chopin's Nocturne in E-flat major, Op. 9, No. 2 played in the background.

In prison blues that clung to his muscular wide body, the ruggedly attractive, Leo looked up at the warden's window from the walking trail and spit as he smoked on his cigarette. "Fucking *suka*. I know that he's looking at me. I can feel it."

"No matter, Boss," one of his lieutenants, Igor said, stretching his sleeve-tattooed arms around and rotating his head in circular motion as they walked. Igor was a red-head with a splash of freckles on his deceptively innocent face but tall and broad with an athletic form that explained why so much damage had been done to the mess hall. Armed with an elementary education and still unable to read or speak much English, Igor was all brawn and no brains.

"What are you doing?" Leo asked with a frown.

"I'm getting ready. Don't want to pull muscle," Igor explained.

"Put your arms down," Leo ordered, swatting at him. "You look like an idiot."

"I just want to be... "

"Igor... " Leo warned, pointing a sharp, thick index finger at him. "Now is not the time."

Igor tucked his head and dropped his arms.

Oleg, Leo's second-in-charge, put his hand on his little brother's shoulder and snickered. "Patience, Igor. You'll get your chance."

When the men made their way around the walking trail to the east side of the wall, they stopped abruptly.

"Was it here or over there?" Igor asked, looking around.

"Here," Leo answered sternly. "Don't move a muscle."

Noticing something was off about the huddle, one of the guards approached cautiously. "Hey," he said, holding on to his asp baton. "Move it along. Keep walking. You only got a few minutes out here anyway before you're sent back to your cage."

"I have *one* fucking hour in this yard every day!" Leo screamed in a raised voice. His anger was unmistakable. "And I've only used 10 minutes of my time. You dumb bastards don't know the difference between 10 minutes and 60?"

"Keep talking, jack off! And we're only going to cut your time shorter," the guard promised. "Now, keep it moving!"

Suddenly the guard stopped as a siren went off above them and guards around the walls began to rally. He looked up in disbelief and heard what sounded like missiles scudding through the air right before a powerful explosion erupted dead in the center of the fortified wall.

Debris shattered outward in every angle along with a plume of smoke and fire.

"Holy shit!" the guard screamed as he hit the ground and covered his head.

Out of the blast zone by only a few feet, Leo stood with his men untouched. "Whose time is being cut short now?" he asked the man as he winked. "Send your warden my regards!"

Gunshots rang out in the yard as more brick was blown from the wall and a missile was launched into the grounds. Hard hitting machine guns specially fitted for the fixed-wing aircraft were let loose on the guards. Their bodies flew off the balconies with gaping holes in them and covered in blood. Bullet holes the size of half dollars filled the side of the prison, while the men in the aircraft laid cover from both sides of the helicopter's open doors.

The wind picked up under the helicopter and dust and dirt swirled about on the ground, making it hard to see anyone. All of Leo's small crew of five looked up as a ladder was thrown from the helicopter down to them.

"One at a time," Oleg said to everyone. He turned to his best friend. "You first, Boss.

Grabbing Oleg by the back of the neck, Leo pushed their heads together. "Thieves-in-Law," he said before he released him.

"Thieves-in-Law!" Oleg said, urging him to climb the ladder to the helicopter. "Hurry, we don't have much time."

As quickly as his strong arms could carry him and his legs could push off from one rung to the other, Leo moved up into the helicopter, praying to miss the flying bullets and hoping not to get caught. There would never be another opportunity like this one. He had to take it. He had to succeed no matter the odds.

One of the men, on the gun on the right side of the helicopter helped him in and locked him in a seat.

"Help my men up!" Leo screamed as the shooting continued in both directions.

"No sir. Just you," the man screamed back as he leaned in and touched the pilot. "Let's move out!"

The helicopters made a sharp left and moved quickly toward the trees in the distance.

"What the fuck do you mean *just me*?" Leo screamed, trying to unlock himself from the seat. "My men are back there!"

Quickly, the gunman put his hand over Leo's hand forcefully. "The warden said *just you*!" He narrowed his eyes and snarled. "Don't look a fucking gift horse in the mouth."

Leo was in disbelief. *If his men didn't go then neither could he.* His mind had already processed the idea of jumping out of the helicopters back down on the ground. Broken bones would be better than stabbing his men in the back. But the gunman must have also seen his intentions and been prepared for them. Reaching into the side pocket of his pants, he pulled out a needle.

"Hold him down," the gunman said to the other man on the other side of the helicopter.

They both jumped with all their weight onto Leo to hold him down while one of them stuck a needle into his neck.

"Ahh!" Leo screamed. "You motherfuckers. I'm going to kill both of you... all of you!"

"There. That should hold him over for a few hours," one of the men said, getting to his feet.

When he was released, Leo immediately felt the effects. Heat rushed through his body, coursing through his veins like venom. Then suddenly everything blurred. Reaching for his seatbelt one last time, he lost consciousness as the aircraft moved quickly away from the prison.

Memphis, TN
Mother Russia Restaurant

In the authentic Russian restaurant known for its infamous history of crime and crime lords through the years, a packed house of curious visitors willing to pay top dollar sat in the main hall enjoying delicious, customary eastern bloc cuisine like Blinchik, Kulebiaka, Chicken Tabaka and Golden Osetra caviar, sampling a variety of vodkas and listening to a Russian folk band flown in from Moscow as they sang the popular folk song *Dark Eyes*.

Lined with expensive green and red intricate rugs flown from St. Petersburg and elaborate paintings from Moscow, the showplace had made the cover of many magazines. Tiffany stained-glass windows, dark hardwood floors, tall ceilings painted in gold with elegantly carved wooden walls and gold-embossed cherubs, red leather booths and tables topped with white linen and candles in golden globes made Mother Russia a unique work of art and a one-of-a-kind eating experience, but it was the owner who made it truly unforgettable.

Dmitry Medlov, a quiet, seven-foot billionaire who had made an excessive amount of front page newspapers himself over the years, had long since retreated to a quiet and very private life hidden behind an entourage of protective bodyguards, but he still gave appearance daily when he popped by his restaurant, usually to go to the secluded rooms in the back for lunch or dinner.

Sightings were always posted on Facebook. People begged for selfies as he passed by or snapped clandestine photos with their phones while they were supposed to be enjoying their meal.

Every once in a while, he even stopped by a few tables just to say a friendly *Allo*, which was hello in his native Russian language, always shocking his patrons to a point of no words. They stared at him in awe of both his dramatic size and unsettling beauty. Women felt overwhelmed. Men felt under achieved and sometimes flat out ugly.

It was as if Michelangelo himself had carved the man's face out of stone and painted it the most beautiful shades of flawless tanned skin, brilliantly honey gold blond hair, startlingly crystal blue eyes and wide, pink lips covering pearly white teeth. And no one could deny his signature smell, an intoxicating and no doubt customized sandalwood, subdued cinnamon and mint. Like a drug, when he passed a woman, she was left with her eyes closed and mouth open, chomping at the bit for just one more interaction.

However, there was never any more than one sighting of the giant by most. Dmitry's schedule could never be truly pinpointed. His head of security saw to that ensuring him and his family's safety.

However, no matter how low key he tried to be, he, his son and his empire were still the topic of polite and impolite conversation in the city of Memphis. The Medlov Organized Crime Family had chosen this small metro to settle down in for good and could not be uprooted even by the most persistent of law enforcement agencies. Because no one could ever prove a case against him, he had become a thing of urban legend, making it unclear if the stories were true or not.

What most people did not recognize, despite the evidence before them, was that the stories were not only true but also very much watered down. The gory details of their real underworld dealings were never revealed to the public, because Dmitry never left a witness to tell the story.

Dmitry Medlov and the Medlov Crime Family were not only the most powerful Russian mafia group in the country, they were also the most deadly. However, because of their legitimate business ties and their governmental influence, they had also become known as untouchable.

And tonight, while couples paid unforgivable prices to dine at their infamous restaurant, pop the question and celebrate promotions, the real men behind the vast empire met in the bowels of the building in a reinforced steel basement to talk about their international trafficking.

The small council was a select group of men in the Medlov Crime Family, who met quarterly to discuss the inner workings of a multinational gun and jewels trafficking business. Among them were Dmitry Medlov, his son Anatoly Medlov and his nephew, Gabriel Medlov.

While sipping vodka and mulling over digital files that showed seven-digit dividends, they mapped out how the deals that they were working on would be planned out for the upcoming quarter.

In the corner, watching their every move and every move that happened on the floors above them through a closed-circuit camera system embedded into the wall was their most trusted bodyguard and head of security, Vasily Kavlov.

Vasily was a quiet man of questionable origins, one of the many reasons that he'd become more like family to the Medlov's than a simple captain. He was shorter than the seven-foot Czar, but a few feet taller than his immediate Boss, Anatoly. However, his body builder physique was no less menacing. He had a prison build from years of working in the gym not only to maintain his size but also to strengthen his lungs, which had been punctured over 10 years ago by Leo Rasputin's bodyguard.

Women always noticed him, despite how invisible he tried to be. With a pensive stare, tanned skin, a low black haircut that he'd recently grown and symmetrically attractive features, Vasily was by all accounts attractive. However, not once was he ever seen with a woman. His black-as-night past only made him more alluring, but even when advanced, he never showed interest.

A feared, revered henchman of the Vory v Zakone, all Vasily had ever known for the last eight years was in this room. He had served the most powerful men in the mafia and his reputation had been nearly flawless doing so. He had killed more men than he cared to count. Done more deals for his bosses then he would ever say. And he had done it all without ever seeking anything in return, except once, *and he had learned that lesson painfully*.

Quietly, with arms crossed over his wide, cement chest, he listened to chatter on his earpiece of guards around the perimeter checking in while at the same time listening to every detail of his boss, Anatoly Medlov's game plan.

"Our men in Kiev have a serious advantage," Anatoly said, sitting back in his chair. He also had a Russian accent and hailed from the grimy streets of Moscow, though no one could tell from the looks of him. He ran a hand through his blonde locks and sighed. "At least until Putin and the UN come to some understanding. Right now, the people who are planning their uprising have been purchasing our munitions in bulk to fight the Ukrainian and Russian army."

Dmitry, sitting at the head of the large antique table, poured himself another glass of water in his crystal goblet. "Don't raise the prices," he ordered. "Right now, we do better to gain their trust. This uprising might not be successful for them, but it won't go away overnight. To price gouge them now would surely turn them to other means."

Anatoly rolled his eyes. "But right now we are making 2-1 for every gun sold," he said, biting his rose-colored lips in frustration. Blue eyes narrowed, he pushed away the iPad "We stand to make more money off of them now... more than we ever have."

For Anatoly, everything came down to money, nothing more.

Dmitry raised a hand to quiet his son and tilted his head. He could already see where Anatoly was going. "This problem won't go away. Our friends in Kiev need to know that we can be trusted with their best interests. Lower the prices and let them know that we are sympathetic to their cause. It will be more profitable in the end."

"We are not freedom fighters," Anatoly grunted. "We are businessmen."

Gabriel, in his normal fashion, listened quietly and neutrally but with a stern glare warned his cousin of challenging Dmitry with such blatant disregard.

Anatoly could feel his cousin's urging but chose to ignore it.

"Do you actually need to tell me what we are, Anatoly?" Dmitry asked. His deep baritone echoed throughout the room. Placing both of his elbows on the table, he clasped his large hands together to relieve some growing agitation. "What do you know of wars, really? You're a young man, who has never had to walk through city streets that were lined with dead bodies. For people who depend on our guns to stay alive, we are nothing if not freedom fighters."

"I don't take sides, Father. You taught me that. I focus on the deal. If it makes sense financially, then it is the right thing to do. If we lose money, then I am opposed. My position has been the same for the whole of my life as a Vor."

Dmitry looked down the table at his ambitious son and sighed. He knew Anatoly's heart and knew that it would take more than a conversation to change it. "Then I pray you live long enough to see that there is more in life than the immediate bottom line. These things take time."

"The war will be over soon. Putin's men are on the border and ready to invade. They won't last against the entire Russian army." Anatoly shook his head. "We should make as much money as we can now."

He had heard enough from his son. "What are your thoughts, Gabriel?" Dmitry asked his nephew.

Gabriel, a mossy green-eyed man nearly as tall as his uncle with ink black hair and his father's ruggedly handsome face, cracked a smile despite his desire not to be put in the middle of the discussion. His American accent always stuck out in conversations. It was distinctly east coast and reeking of privileged private schools and Ivy League colleges. "I don't agree with Anatoly on this. I think we should lower the prices to help them, but I also don't agree with you completely, uncle. *No disrespect.* We should tell them that the prices will rise after the conflict. However, considering every dollar matters now, we will work with them. We prove our loyalty on the front end, but we also ensure that at some point, we recoup any losses."

Anatoly, for once, could see logic in his cousin's reasoning. He flexed his fingers. "He might just be a Medlov after all," he quipped.

Dmitry raised a brow. "And what will make them stay with us after the conflict, if we tell them that we will raise the prices after the war, even if they lose?"

"The same loyalty that we have shown them, of course," Gabriel answered with a frown. *Was that not obvious?*

Dmitry laughed and slapped his hand on the table truly amused. "Good luck with that." He pushed away his paper file. "Very well. You two will never learn if I don't let you make your own deals. Do this your way, but if they don't win, and they don't come back to us after the conflict, then the both of you will pay any losses out of your own pockets. And based upon these projections in this file, that's a lot of money. 2-1 is what you said, right Anatoly?"

"That is over two million dollars... American dollars," Anatoly huffed. "Each quarter." He looked over at Gabriel as if to tell him that he'd blown it.

"Well, let us hope that you are right," Dmitry said softly. "Otherwise, you will both be two million dollars lighter *every single* quarter if you are wrong. We have a deal with people leading a revolution in the 8th largest country in Europe. To fuck it up is unacceptable. You will not learn how to deal with global conflicts on my dime. If you are wise enough to do things your way, then you will be wise enough to pay the consequences *if* things don't turn out the way that you predict." He gave an easy smile. "But I trust your decision. And I have faith that you won't end up two million dollars poorer... per quarter until you find someone to replace the account."

"Of course," Anatoly said, rolling his eyes again. "The old man has figured out a way to make his money no matter what. Do you see this, Gabriel? This is the reward we get for trying to save a dollar for him."

Dmitry laughed again. "This is the price of being a boss."

"I never asked to be a boss," Gabriel said, putting his head in his hands. "You people are unreal. Aren't you the Czar? Shouldn't you make the final call?"

Dmitry raised a brow. "It's your legacy. When I'm dead and gone, you still have to take care of this family. If you have to pay, consider it money going into a long-term savings account."

"Oh, well that's comforting, considering how many children the Medlov men seem to put out a year, by the time you die, we'll be in debt," Gabriel said under his breath.

Pulling out his phone, Anatoly checked his email and then huffed. "Shit," he said, grabbing the remote for the large television across the room. "Looks like there is a problem in New York."

"What now?" Dmitry asked with a frown.

Turning on the television, Anatoly quickly turned to a cable network where breaking news from Attica flashed across the screen. A woman stood in front of a burning wall of the prison reporting that Russian mob boss Leo Rasputin had broken out of prison and a national manhunt led by US Marshalls was underway.

Stepping out of the shadows Vasily walked over to the television and listened carefully. His brow furrowed and heat started to form under his perfectly pressed collar. "Boss," he said, turning back to Anatoly with concern.

Anatoly wiped his face and then stood up. He walked over to his father, leaned down and whispered something in his ear, leaving the rest of the men puzzled.

Dmitry listened and nodded his head. "Vasily, you may take your leave."

"Thank you," Vasily said, gratefully.

"How long will you need?" Anatoly asked. His tone was amazingly filled with unease.

"At most two days. I'll know more when I get there," Vasily said, pointing at one of his other men. "Boris will watch over you while I'm gone."

Boris quickly took his boss's lead. "I'm ready," he assured him.

"Call us should you need anything? Stop by the house. Get what you need from the safe," Anatoly said, looking at his watch. "Do you need a plane?"

"Yes, Boss," Vasily answered, walking to the door. "I appreciate this."

"There is no need to thank us. You are family," Dmitry reminded.

Nodding Vasily put his code into the padlocked door and unlocked it.

Within minutes, he was up the private elevator and onto the main floor of the restaurant with the rest of the crowds of people, who were eating, dancing and laughing. He moved quickly through the huddles of clueless masses, making sure to be careful not to let anyone brush past the guns in the holsters under his arms as they swarmed the corridor.

As the hostess opened the front door for him, he stepped out into the night air, entering an abrupt and welcomed silence of night. There in the front on the cobblestone street a black S-class Mercedes Benz waited on him. The driver nodded and opened the back door for him.

"Where to, sir?" the driver asked as Vasily stepped inside.

"Back to the compound," Vasily said, looking at his watch. Each moment was precious. He had to hurry.

Chapter 2

The heavy rains of a hot summer's night didn't seem to keep people out of the small back road bar that Lilly worked in on Saturdays. It was packed way past fire code with every blue collar worker in the area ordering a beer and unwinding after a long day at the job.

Country music played on the jukebox; people played pool and others drank and played darts. In the seedy corners, couples kissed and hugged while a few argued over the news. In all, it truly was an average Saturday of *normal* proportions.

In a pair of worn sneakers, short shorts that showed the pockets from the bottoms and a white t-shirt that put her large bosom on display with the word *Cleveland* across the back in fire engine red, Lilly ran in between tables serving up big mugs of beer on tap and typical pub crawl food while swatting hands that tried desperately to feel her up.

"I hate my life," she said, resting against the bar while the bartender, Logan, loaded up her round wooden tray again. She stepped back a millimeter and wiped the front of her clothes were a beer had spilled on the bar and was dripping off the side. "Great!" she cursed. "That's just great."

"Well, sweetheart, things could always be worse," Logan said, with a trace of humor in his lusty hazel eyes. "Give me a kiss. It might make you feel better," he said, reaching over the bar to grab her face jokingly.

"In your dreams, Logan," Lilly said, snatching back. "Everyone knows that you're a pig."

"A reputation that I don't deserve," Logan explained with a toothy grin. He gave her a suggestive wink, one that he had given her every night since the first night that she'd started working there. Unfortunately, his country boy good looks didn't work on her, nor did the Wrangler jeans, the Timberland boots or his signature pearly white t-shirt that showed off his meaty, former football playing pecks.

"A reputation that you've worked hard to uphold from what I've heard," she said as she picked up her tray. The moisture below the tray from the wet bar made her fingers slip slightly. Still, she gripped it tightly.

"Well, I'd turn in my card for you, Lilly you Northern Belle," he promised. "I'd marry you at the chapel on Saturday, and give you a bunch of babies on Sunday morning, darlin'."

"Pity your *momma* doesn't like black women," Lilly snickered. "I don't believe that I'm the right shade to be Mrs. Mosby."

"It's the 20th century," Logan said, hitting his broad chest. "I can change."

"21st century," Lilly corrected. "You are about a hundred years behind as is the rest of this shit hole." She joked with him, but she meant it wholeheartedly. She absolutely abhorred Jackson, Mississippi.

Logan laughed. "It's that kind of attitude that's gonna keep you single, Lilly."

"Single isn't a bad thing in comparison to a bad relationship. Trust me," she said with a wry smile.

In his normal chauvinistic fashion, he watched her backside as she walked away. Licking his lips, he shook his head. "Damn, girl."

Lilly walked over to her normal guys who worked for the railroad and put their drinks on the table, when she noticed the news on the television above them. A flash of Attica Prison drew her attention.

"How ya doing there, good looking," Greg said, taking his glass off the tray. "I've been dreaming about this drink all damn day. Dear God, Lilly. You are a life saver."

Normally, Lilly would have had a quirky comeback, but at the moment, she was paralyzed. Staring at the television as the words Leo Rasputin flashed across the ticker below a reporter, she broke out in a cold sweat.

"Something wrong?" Greg asked, noticing her sudden change.

The room began to swim.

Lilly swallowed down a fleeting breath. Her heart thudded in her chest. "Just... the damn news." She tried to laugh, but it came across with the same nervousness as her broken face. "I'll be right back, boys," she said, nearly falling over her own feet.

It was as if she were walking in a fog. With hands shaking, he found her way back to the bar. "Hey Logan, I need to go," she said, palms flat on the wet bar, forgetting its stickiness.

"What?" He frowned. "I'm already short. Lisa won't be here for another hour."

"I'm sorry," Lilly said absently before she darted to the back. "I've got to go."

Logan was quickly behind her. "What's going on? What's wrong?" He grabbed her arm and swung her around. "Jeez, you're shaking like a leaf. What happened back there? Did Greg say something to you? I'll beat his ass."

Lilly looked away. "No. It's not Greg. I just need to go, Logan. And I need to go *right now*."

Seeing that she was clearly in no state to serve his customers, he let her arm go. "Well, is there anything that I can do?"

"No," she said, grabbing her purse out of her locker. "I appreciate it."

"Well, can you at least tell me what's going on?"

"Just felt sick all of a sudden. Like something I ate. It just hit me," she lied.

"Something here?" He probed.

Lilly felt her stomach cramp. "I'm going to be sick," she said, running toward the employee restroom. Closing the door behind her, she fell on her knees in front of the toilet.

Logan could hear her throwing up as he pressed his head to the door. All suspicion quailed; he put his hand on the door in the truest of sympathy. "Get better. Do you need me to drive you home?"

Wiping her mouth, Lilly held on to the cool seat of the toilet. "No, I'll be fine. I'm just going to slip out the back door and head home, okay?"

"Yeah, sure. No worries," Logan said, still unsure if he should leave her alone. "Call me if you need anything."

"Okay," Lilly said, wiping tears from her eyes. She tried to still her quivering voice.

Getting up off her knees and flushing the toilet, she looked at herself in the mirror above the sink. Suddenly, she had gone pale, despite her warm brown skin.

It only took one man's name to do her in.

Running water in the sink, she washed her face to cool her burning cheeks and pulled her hair down out of the two ponytails. Digging for a brush in her purse, she quickly combed her hair down and grabbed her keys. She had to get a handle on herself now.

***

When Leo came out of his deep sleep, he realized that he was no longer in the helicopter used to help him escape the prison but in a dark room in a real bed, *something that he had been denied for many years*. His body was absorbed by the softness of the mattress.

He relished in its comfort until finally fully awake, he sat up in the bed and looked around. It took a minute for his eyes to adjust to the pitch blackness.

Focusing on the light coming from under the door and the moonlight coming from the window, he stood up still in his prison uniform and went to the door.

After many years of being told what to do every second of his life, he felt nervous about simply opening the door on his own. A wave of distrust came over him, and he put his head on the door to listen to the muffled voices on the other side.

The echo of deep, laughing Russian accents calmed him.

Finally opening the door, his eyes squinted at the overwhelming light on the other side of the dark room. He walked slowly out, cautiously looking around.

As he emerged, his men stopped talking and stood up.

One of his closest men before the arrests was standing only feet away from him.

"," Aleksi said with a nervous smile. "You finally got up. We thought that you'd sleep all night."

Leo looked around at all his men. There wasn't a face in the room that he didn't recognize making him feel as though he was at a reunion of sorts. "Yes, I'm finally awake," he said, scratching his stubbly beard. Next thing he'd get a good shave from a barber, but for now... "Where are we?" he asked.

"Ottawa," Aleksi explained. "Canada."

"Is there another Ottawa?" Leo asked sarcastically. *Fucking yahoo.*

Aleski shrugged his shoulders. He didn't know one way or the other. "We had to get you out of the country, ASAP. You're all over the news like a fucking movie star. Police are looking everywhere. We smuggled you here in a box when you were dropped off by that warden's men."

Leo smiled and rolled his large arm in a circular motion. "That explains the soreness. I feel like I was hit by a truck." He walked over to the table and all the food that had been prepared. There was plenty of meat, potatoes, cabbage and beer. "This for me?" he asked, mouthwatering and stomach growling.

A big smile appeared. "*Da, da*, boss. We wanted to give you the best homecoming we could. All your favorites are here in one big meal." Reaching under the table, Aleski pulled out a case and opened it, revealing two custom-made Glocks. "You remember these? We managed to save them from the Feds." He offered them proudly.

Leo ran his hand over the cold steel and shook his head. "Oh, I remember everything," he said, picking one of the guns up. He took a fully loaded magazine and shoved it into the Glock until it made a distinctive click and sighed. It was like music to his ears. "Now, that feels good," he said with a wicked grin.

All five of the men at the table laughed.

Leo scratched his naturally arched eyebrow with the muzzle of the gun and squinted as he recalled something disturbing. "You know, it's funny. I don't remember what a hot bath feels like, what a good meal or a good fuck feels like, but I do remember what stab right in the back feels like. It's a very sobering thing."

The tension in the room began to heighten.

Aleski looked over at his boss confused. "What?" he asked, paying closer attention to Leo now that he was armed.

"I paid a lot of money to that prick of a lawyer Lowenstein. And he promised me one thing; if he couldn't get me off, he'd damn sure make me aware of everyone who had put me there. And one of those reports guess whose name showed up for giving information to the fucking cops during an investigation on me?" he said, still sort of chuckling.

The tension in the room heightened. Four of the five men looked at their friend in disbelief.

"You helped keep me locked up like a fucking animal, Aleski, just so you could become boss of my men."

Aleski frowned in confusion. "Who me?" He touched his chest. "Not me. No, boss. I never gave anyone nothing. I'm telling you. Someone is lying."

Leo laughed. "Oh really? Then how are you walking like a free man? I mean, I know how Yakov is. He managed to get to the only guy who could testify against him and cut his balls off. And we thought that we had taken care of everyone else but it stuck. Why did the charge stick?"

"I don't know. I ain't no fucking lawyer," Aleksi said, sweat pouring over his face.

"It stuck because you and that bitch made it stick," Leo growled.

Before Aleksi could respond, Leo raised his gun quickly and pulled the trigger twice. Each shot rang into the large man, sending him backwards and onto the floor. Before Aleksi's eyes could dim, Leo stepped over him and shot him again in the chest.

"*Suka*," Leo said, spitting on Aleksi's carcass.

When he finished, he turned to the other men in the room who stood stupefied by the act as if nothing had happened. Suddenly, the darkness in his eyes had lifted and he almost had a grin tugging at the sides of his mouth. Still, no one knew if they would be next. They all froze in place, waiting to see what the verdict would be.

"Now that that's done, we can relax. I don't remember anyone else's name, so by all means, sit down. Eat with me," he said, pulling back Aleksi's chair. "Come, come." He kicked the dead man's leg out of the way and sat down at the table, ready to enjoy his feast.

His men, unable and unwilling to speak, did the same. To say that they were completely surprised by his actions would have been a lie. Boss Leo had never been a man of many words, but murder was a typical action that he seemed to carry out with a certain amount of unforgiveable pleasure.

As they ate and drank above the dead man's body, they all tried to avoid any looks of loss for their friend, or they knew that they would possibly tempt their boss. Remorse was not taken lightly. And what was done, was done.

Assessing the heightened fear permeating the room, Leo took a deep breath of it and continued. "Now," Leo said, grabbing a turkey leg off the platter across from him. "Let's talk about how to get me back into the U.S. and to find that whore of an ex-wife of mine, kill her and get my fucking diamonds back so that I can actually get on with building my empire back up."

One of his other men spoke up. "Boss, the U.S. is too hot right now. We should be getting you to Venezuela like we planned where there is no extradition. If we go back, you could get caught. Is there any way that we can do this for you? Surely we can find her."

Leo hit the table in anger, knocking glasses of wine over and down onto the floor. Voice raised, he spat out angry words. "I'm flat fucking broke right now besides a couple of hundred thousand dollars, I had stashed away. I went from millions on top of millions to damn near nothing because of a few motherfuckers and their testimonies, even my own wife, who divorced me in prison and ran off with $20 million in uncut diamonds. Well now, I want her head on a plate," he growled. "And I want those diamonds back in my hand. And no one is going anywhere or doing anything else until

Lilly Rasputin is hunted down. Do I make myself clear?"

He looked around the table at nodding or bowed heads. No one wanted to make eye contact, especially about the present topic. Lilly was a touchy subject, one that no one wanted to broach. Evidently, she had married him despite a falling out about a former bodyguard. However, she turned against him like a rattlesnake as soon as the fed's came knocking, when she could have taken the 5th and never given them a thing.

Sitting back, he relaxed his broad shoulders. "Now, the way I figure it, I can make my way to find the man who last saw her alive. Find Yakov. He hasn't been to see me once in Attica. Word is that he went soft, started a family in Brighton Beach. He shouldn't be too hard to find, and if I know him, he knows exactly where she is."

Chapter 3

In a broke down 1998 blue Honda Accord with paint chips missing and a loud muffler, Lilly zoomed up her long, dirt driveway kicking up dust and mud to her home, an old 1930's style, two-story, white wood house with a wraparound porch and a swing. She had a Coltrane CD blasting to drown out the irritatingly loud sound of her busted car and the windows down to make up for the air conditioner on the fritz.

One could tell that in its glory, the old home used to be a beautiful testament to fine living, but now it was shabby and in need of serious power washing. Still, it was more than she could have ever hoped after her split with Leo.

By all accounts, she should have been dead, locked in a barrel full of acid and discarded in the Hudson River, but she had been saved, yet again.

It had been a turn of luck that she had not expected, but each and every day since that day, she had thanked God for life and tried to live it with full appreciation.

And how could she not?

The night that Vasily ran up the stairs of Leo's home to stop him from beating her, she thought that he was surely dead when Leo's man shot him. Only the bullet that went through his body didn't kill him. His friend, Yakov, got him to an underground doctor that removed the bullet and put him up for a few weeks until he could get out of New York and down south to a man named Anatoly who gave him a job.

Unfortunately, she didn't know that Vasily was alive until a couple of months after she and Leo were married.

It had been a bad idea to become his wife, but one that she had little choice in. Prior to being convicted on money laundering, violating the RICO Act and first degree murder charges, Leo was in the country on a work visa from Moscow. He had been using that visa for years until Immigration and Customs Enforcement started to dig into his international business dealings. As soon as his visa lapsed, they threatened to send him back to Moscow. A move he could not afford because of his enemies there. His solution to the problem was an elaborate wedding to her.

She wanted to say no for all the moral reasons to Leo, but for the immoral ones that all included millions of dollars and a comfortable lifestyle, she had agreed.

She would never forget the night that he took her to dinner at the Russian Tea Room in Manhattan and over a candlelit dinner in the famous Bear Lounge proposed that they get married for all the wrong reasons and learn to love each other for the right ones. In truth, she knew that he was lying. He had no intention of loving her, and she had no intention of loving him. She just didn't want to give up her lifestyle. Plus, she knew that if she turned him down, with all that she had seen and all that she knew, he would kill her. Having his last name was her life insurance policy.

After the pseudo-proposal, she got a huge engagement ring to show off to the other mob wives and girlfriends, followed by a car with a driver and a Black American Express card.

Life was good for a minute. But after the newness of marriage wore off, Leo forgot his promise to never hit her again. Then the real Leo came back out, and being slapped around became a normal occurrence, only there was no Vasily to make it stop.

Life for Lilly became unbearable. In just a short time, she went from loving being Mrs. Rasputin to contemplating suicide to end it all. She prayed to God for an answer, begged Him to forgive her for marrying for the wrong reasons and even tried walking on egg shells around her husband. Nothing worked.

She was just about to look into poisoning him when God finally heard her prayers.

Normally, Leo had men who would tip him off when the Feds were sniffing around, but he hadn't been informed about the latest and most serious set of charges that he was being brought up on by the U.S. District Attorney. They came in the middle of the night. Swift and hard, they pounced on their brownstone and arrested everyone except for her and Yakov, who was spared because he was not at the house that night.

In a drastic and desperate move, as the Feds came up the stairs to their bedroom after him, Leo gave Lilly a bag of diamonds that he had just heisted to hide for him until he returned. She had hidden them in her bra, under her ample breasts. When the Feds came barreling through the door and saw her in her night clothes, they gave her enough privacy in the corner to get dressed. That kindness ultimately allowed her to hide the precious stones better.

They took Leo with them, handcuffed and cursing.

They left her there with $20 million in untraceable diamonds.

Shortly after that, she sought her opportunity to get revenge on Leo for killing Vasily and testified against him in court. The DA was hounding her for her testimony, especially since all of the witnesses kept being murdered. She was sure that Yakov had a hand in it because he was the only one who wasn't in jail, but she was not absolutely sure until the night he came calling late with a blade in his hand, if she was in danger.

She convinced him that it was worth his while not to kill her. And they made a deal—a quiet one that only the two of them knew about.

Once convicted, the DA managed to find a way to take everything from Leo including the brownstone, all the cars, the jewelry and the money, but they didn't get the diamonds.

Hours after his sentencing, she was smuggled out of the city by Yakov and taken to Memphis where she saw Vasily for the first time since that dreadful night.

Yakov handed her over to him and said goodbye forever. Vasily took her deep into Mississippi, a place where credit was not necessarily a necessity and black women were never expected to be the wives of crime lords. She was damn near invisible, just the way she needed to be. She took a job in a roadhouse, got rid of all airs and became a completely new woman.

Here she made her life, one that included nothing from her past... *well almost nothing.*

After he left her, Vasily never checked on her or gave any indication that he remembered who or where she was. In fact, he had explained that that would be her sign that everything was safe.

As long as he didn't come around, and as long as there was absolutely no communication, it meant that Leo was still in jail and still worlds away from her.

Now with Leo's breakout, nothing and no one would be safe. She had to get out of here quick. Besides, considering all the time that had passed Vasily had probably moved on with his life and forgotten about her.

Pulling up to the front door of her home, she turned off her loud car, grabbed her purse from the passenger seat and jumped out.

She knew that she didn't have a lot of time.

Bolting up the stairs in nearly a sprint, she slipped her keys into the wide oak door and pushed it open. Wind chimes jingled on the porch in the wind as she closed the door behind her. Normally, the sound was inviting, but tonight, it sent chills down her spine.

In pitch black with only the street light outside to guide her through the foyer, she moved quickly to the living room lamp to turn it on, but felt someone move from out of the shadows and grab her from behind.

The large arms were strong and unforgiving. With a hand across her mouth to keep her screams muffled, she felt the strange embrace pull her into his body. Only it wasn't rough or threatening.

"Shh," he whispered in her ear. "Leave the lamp off. We don't know who is watching."

Even as her body shook in fear, the sound of his voice soothed her. She knew the voice and suddenly remembered the touch. Her hand that had been pushing the arm away from her waist, suddenly stroked it. She could feel the muscles in his forearm and feel the scars that she had memorized over ten years ago.

Slowly, he removed his hand from her mouth and allowed her to turn slightly to see his face. Seeing him in the flesh after all those years literally made her heart skip a beat. He was even more beautiful now.

Without thought, she grabbed him and hugged him tightly, soaking up his body heat and melting into his muscles. "Vasily," she whispered, head pressed against his chest.

Vasily wasn't expecting the warm welcome but he couldn't deny that he enjoyed it. He held her tight and closed his eyes. Thank God she was okay. Still here. Still safe.

"Lilly," he answered in a low baritone. "I didn't mean to scare you."

The release was painful. As he moved away, she took a deep breath. "I'm just glad it's you."

Vasily's eyes flickered like diamonds in the light coming through the windows. His mouth curved into words like he was fighting saying something, but a flash of sanity made him push whatever was on the tip of his tongue back to the recesses of his mind.

Lilly knew that look. He was shutting down. Redirecting to kill the awkwardness, she moved on to more pressing issues. "How long have you been here waiting on me?" she said, praying that he didn't hear the thud of her anxious heartbeat.

"I just arrived about five minutes before you." He stepped closer to the window and looked out again.

"How did you get in?" she frowned.

He raised a brow. "Really?"

She couldn't help but crack a sideways smile, despite the situation. "It's been a while. Forgive me. I forget who I am talking to."

Her smile did something to him, even in this situation. He quietly admired her warm face.

She was just as beautiful as the day that he had left her here.

He nodded and kept his voice pitched low. "We don't have a lot of time. I need you to get a bag and be ready to go in five minutes. My car is around the back of the house. I'll take you to a private air strip… "

Lilly shook her head, cutting him off. "We have one more stop to make before we leave here then."

"We don't have time for any stops," he urged. "I can't be certain what Leo's intentions are. He could already be in another country or right around the corner. Until I can figure out what is going on, you're not safe."

Lilly's chest tightened, but she managed to get the words out. "I have to get my son. He's at the babysitter's house. He stays there whenever I'm at work." Her eyes bounced about, unable to look straight at him.

Vasily froze like a snapshot. "Son?" he asked.

Lilly nodded. "My son," she repeated. She finally looked at him and exhaled a deep breath.

Vasily licked his lips and took a step back. *He wasn't expecting that.* "Where is the father? Is he going to be a problem?"

"No," she said softly. Her eyes darted again, this time catching Vasily's attention, though he said nothing.

He nodded abruptly, trying to hide his disappointment. "Good, well then… " He looked toward the hallway. "Let's hurry and get your *son*."

***

As Vasily had instructed, Lilly left her old battered car in the driveway and made the house look as though she and her son were there. However, even though she was glad to be getting some help, it still felt odd for Lilly to leave her home after so many years.

She tried hard to hide her anxiety as she rode in the car with Vasily. In a state of silent panic, she swallowed down the tears as she watched her home fade in the car's mirrors. She pushed past the pain in her chest when she was forced to leave the photos on the walls and the finger paintings on the refrigerator.

Somewhere during the transition of being a mafia wife to a minimum wage worker, she had grown a lot, seen the many errors in her ways. She was proud now to be her own person and proud to have something to be proud of that wasn't based upon someone else's title or banking account. It had not been easy, but she had survived and now that reality was quickly disappearing.

Not used to the cold air of a luxury car, she opted to let her window down and take in the night air. It blew through her hair and wiped away the excess tears that she couldn't hold back from the corners of her tired eyes. She was expecting Vasily to insist that she let it back up, but he drove quietly, never uttering a word and keeping his eyes on the road.

He's angry, she thought to herself. *He thinks that I've been with someone else.*

She had not.

Not since he touched her all those years ago.

Leo had been a lesson in life about bad men, and Vasily had been a lesson in her life about good ones. Both had left an indelible mark on her, changing her perceptions of relationships forever.

She looked over him, brooding in his prickly exterior, and felt the need to reach out and touch him, to reassure him of her undying love but she did not. She kept her hands balled up in her lap, wishing that he could drive faster to get to her son.

Despite everything else she couldn't help notice that the years had been kind to him. He had aged well, become more beautiful in fact. Well-groomed in his black tailored suit, he looked like a man of means, smelled intoxicatingly masculine. Vasily was regal now, a man who had conquered his fears and the world around him. She could see it in his posture, in his stare.

Feeling her looking at him, Vasily glanced over at her, but she quickly looked away.

After hearing that she was a mother, Vasily stood in the living room in the same spot quietly while she packed a couple of bags and then escorted her out of the back door to his car. Somehow, even though he knew there had been many years put between them, he still was not ready for the news that she had moved on, even for a night.

Seeing her again had been earth-shattering for him. When he had held her in her living room, it had been torture to let go. She felt warm and gentle, just the way that she had felt the first time that he had held her. Being around her had sent him back 10 years in life and suddenly for the first time in a very long time, he felt vulnerable.

He had so many questions. Did she love another man now? Was she leaving someone that she truly cared for? Had he been just an instrument to keep her safe?

His questions were endless and his solitude even more so than the moment that he walked away from her.

As they pulled up to the address that she had put into the GPS, he put the car in park and turned off the lights. Staring at the building, he realized just how poor Lilly was now.

"This it?" he asked as a man with a Colt 45 walked pass the car and looked inside.

With a nod, she opened the door. "I'll be right back."

"I will go with you," he insisted, getting out also.

"Do you think that's wise? You sort of... " She squint her eyes. "Stick out."

"Someone could be in there waiting on you," he said, rubbing his hand over his guns in their holsters. "I can't risk it." Plus, he was used to sticking out, especially in the south.

They walked side-by-side through the low-income apartment complex past the people standing outside congregating under the street lights to a unit on the first floor. It was the only one with a welcome mat out front.

Feeling mildly embarrassed, Lilly rang the doorbell.

An older black woman came to the door with an apron on, holding a small baby in her arms.

Vasily noticed the brown and chubby baby, and wondered if that was Lilly's.

"You're early," the woman said, opening the door so that they could both come in. She gave Vasily a look that he couldn't shake, like she knew him from somewhere.

"Is Dylan still up?" Lilly asked, looking around.

The woman cut a look one more time at Vasily before she answered. "Yes, he's on the couch watching television. He's already eaten and had a bath. I was expecting him to spend the night and go to church with us in the morning."

Lilly looked back at Vasily as he followed her into the small living room. "This is my... " She was lost for an explanation. *Who was he to her anyway?*

"I'm Marcus Weaver," Vasily said in his best American accent. He offered his hand to the woman and gave a deceivingly welcoming smile. "I'm a friend of Lilly's from back home. Where're driving back to New York for a family member's funeral."

"I'm Maxine Clemmons," the woman said, shaking his hand gently. She looked over at Lilly. "I've never heard her mention any family to speak of."

Lilly's mouth dropped open at Vasily's accent. Nearly speechless, she blinked hard. "Yes," she said, clearing her throat. She tried to focus, to speak up. Ms. Clemmons wouldn't believe them otherwise. "Well, I'm not really close with my family, but I felt like I should go pay my respects. We'll be gone for about a week." She looked back up at Vasily.

"Give or take," Vasily added. "There will be a will to review. She has quite a sizeable inheritance coming to her."

"Oh. Well, I'm sorry for your loss," Ms. Clemmons said to Lilly. Moving the baby to her other hip, she called into the next room. "Dylan, grab your backpack. Your mother is here."

Vasily's curiosity peaked. *The child on the old woman's hip wasn't Lilly's? How old was her son?*

A moment later a young boy, around eight years old, came around the corner in a pair of jeans and a red t-shirt with his backpack hanging off one arm.

He was tall for his age with a wide, healthy build. He had curly chocolate locks, fair skin, rose-colored cheeks and lips and bright green eyes the color of jade.

"Hey, mom," he said, walking up to her and hugging her around her waist.

"Hey, baby," she said, kissing the crown of his head.

Dylan looked over at Vasily and tilted his head. "Who's that?" he asked.

Lilly looked up at Vasily, seeing the shock paralyze him. "That's Mommy's old friend, Marcus," she said, grabbing his small hand.

Chapter 4

Vasily couldn't breathe. No matter how he tried to take in deep breaths, no matter how much oxygen filled his lungs, he still couldn't breathe.

As he watched Lilly and her son load into his car, he felt like fainting right there in the apartment complex—a first for him in all of his life. He had witnessed and committed murders; he had seen men tortured; he had done unspeakable acts without question, but never in his life had he experienced this.

Lilly closed the back door and looked across at him. "Can we just talk about this in private?" she asked as she studied the range of emotions that were crossing his face.

Vasily leaned both arms over the black Cadillac in utter emotional exhaustion and looked her square in the eye. "Just answer one question for me and we can go. Is he... "

"Yes," she interrupted, unable to wait another second.

"Leo's?" he finished.

"What?" her voice shrieked. "No, of course not. He's... " She huffed. "Isn't it obvious, Vasily?" With a spiked brow, she shook her head and took a deep breath. Rubbing a hand through her hair, she shrugged her thin shoulders. "He's yours," she whispered, afraid her son would hear her.

Vasily bent down and looked into the car's backseat at the boy. As he did, Dylan waved at him and smiled. Quickly he rose back up, and gawked at her. "Why did you not tell me in all these years?" he grunted.

Lilly opened the passenger door and raised a finger. "You said *one question*. I answered it. Now can we go? We can talk more when we are alone *and safe*."

Getting in the car and slamming the door, he pulled off and headed for the private airstrip. Now more intense than ever, he refused to look over at her. A million thoughts assailed him, nearly all at once. But more than that, he worried.

Glancing back in the rearview mirror at the boy, he tried to wrap his mind around the fact that he had fathered a son.

"How could you have done this to me?" he finally asked.

"What?" she said, turning to him.

"I showed you nothing but kindness and you do this?"

Lilly snapped her mouth shut and folded her arms. "Vasily, I didn't tell you for the same reasons that you didn't want to check on me. I didn't want to put him in harm's way. If anyone knew who you were or who he was… " She shook off the thought. "He would have never seen his first birthday."

Despite his growing anger, Vasily tried to keep his voice low. The last thing he wanted to do was scare the boy. *That would just be a great first impression.* Still the point had to be made. "I could have kept him safe. I could have kept you both safe. Besides, in the end, I'm forced to anyway."

Lilly instantly took offense. "You're not forced to do anything. I was going home to pack and leave. We were going to disappear," she said, looking out of the window. "It's not like I called you. You just showed up back there."

"Leo would have found you in days, Lilly." Vasily knuckles turned bone white as he gripped the steering wheel. "He would have done horrible things to you *and him*." Pure evil Vasily remembered of his old boss. "Especially him," he croaked out.

Lilly knew that he was telling the truth. She also knew Vasily coming to get her was a blessing. It was just that it had been so many years since she had been able to depend on any man for anything until it was hard to accept his protection. And she hated herself for it.

Cutting her eyes over to his hands, she twisted up her mouth. "I don't want to fight," she said a little softer. "I never meant for you to find out this way. I had it all played out in my mind and it wasn't like this. You have to believe me."

He took his eyes off the road for a brief moment and looked over at her. He could see the determination in her eyes, the will to survive. *How could he not respect that?* With a nod, he focused back on the road. "*Da, da*. I know."

That small recognition was enough to satis-fy Lilly, if only for the moment. Uncrossing her arms, she reached for the radio. "Do you mind?" she asked. The silence of the ride was forcing her to talk and at the moment that was the last thing that she needed to do. Maybe the music would lighten the mood and give her time to think about something that was not stupid or callous to say.

"Nyeht," Vasily answered. "Help yourself."

As she turned on the radio, she was hit with another untimely coincidence. Marvin Gaye's *Distant Lover* played, taunting them both with not only the gravity of their current situation but also the reminder of how Dylan got here in the first place.

Shaking her head, she sat back in the seat and looked out the window with a conde-scending smirk.

What a day?

***

It was time for his dogs' midnight snack, and he couldn't stand the idea of someone else feeding them. It was his only time to relax and do something that he enjoyed that didn't require an army around him or interaction with other asshole humans.   Anatoly trotted through the carefully manicured grass with his head down, dragging on a cigarette and enjoying the serene peacefulness while making his way to the kennel.

Of course, his men weren't far. They watched him from less than 50 feet away while he went about his business. But at least they were not on his flank, which lately his father preferred.

Anatoly had a rule about his backyard. If his men were close enough to smell a fart, then they were too close. But his father always worried about ambushes and felt that if they were too far away, then they couldn't take a bullet for him. It was two schools of thought. One family. Such was the story of his life.

Boris, the newly in-charge head of security, observed him most intently. There was no way in hell that he was going to let anything happen to his boss on his watch. Instead of hanging back, he walked toward his boss slowly, hoping that he wouldn't notice him closing in.

Anatoly did of course notice, but did not say anything. He had been in Boris' shoes not too long ago in his life and knew what the job was like.

As he opened the kennel, one of his larger German Shepard's leaped out into his arms, excited to see his master after many hours. Hugging and kissing his canine companion, he suddenly felt his phone vibrate in the back pocket of his jeans. Considering his wife, cousin and his father were inside the compound, he was certain it was only one person at this time of night.

"You find her?" he asked as he answered his phone.

Lilly and Dylan were escorted up the steps and then inside the jet as Vasily watched. "Da, boss. But there is a glitch." He smacked his lips together. "She's got a kid."

"How's that a glitch? Just put them both up somewhere until this blows over."

"It's my kid," Vasily answered more specifically.

Anatoly paused. He wanted to laugh at the irony, but opted not to.

"That kind of glitch, eh?" Anatoly took another drag of his cigarette and looked up at the clear night's sky. "Alright. Bring them here."

"Are you sure?" Vasily was expecting to be sent to Miami or even to Denver, but he wasn't expecting his boss to open up his home.

"*Brat*, we're family. Now, if the kid wasn't yours, I'd tell you to take them somewhere else, but... " He hesitated. "Wait, you sure he's yours?" Anatoly couldn't help his cynicism. He didn't trust anyone but family.

"It's a good possibility."

"Does he look like you? Is the timeline right?" Anatoly hated to ask, but he had had more than a few experiences with desperate women and their lies.

"Timeline's right. He looks like his mother." Vasily grunted. "And my father a little."

"Ouch. That's gotta suck," Anatoly cracked. He exhaled a deep breath. "Bring them here. I'll tell Papa. We'll figure out the rest when you get here."

"I can't thank you enough," Vasily answered as a thousand-pound weight lifted off his shoulders.

Anatoly was a little taken back although he didn't say it. Vasily had never once in all of his years said those words to him. "We all have to take care of our own. Besides if my father protected that cop's family a year ago then we damn sure are going to protect our own now."

Vasily brow rose. Anatoly had a point. "I'll be there in two hours," he said, hanging up the phone.

***

It had been a long time since Lilly had been on a jet. She sat back in the white leather seat with her son tucked beside her and waited as the attendant checked to ensure that they were locked in properly. She noticed that even though the blond woman was extremely petite and pretty, she carried weapons in holsters like most women wore earrings.

Graceful in her movements, the flight attendant gave them both warm assuring smiles.

"Would you like anything to drink before we begin take off?" she asked Lilly.

"No," she said, eyeing the guns again. She wasn't sure if she'd be able to explain this to Dylan later. She rubbed his hand. "Are you thirsty, baby?"

"I want a Sprite," Dylan answered. He rested his head on his mother's arm and stared across the plane. "Mommy, I'm scared."

"Why?" she asked, voice pitched high.

"I've never been on a plane before. I'm scared of planes. I saw one on the news that went down in the ocean. Nobody lived," Dylan answered.

It explained why the boy hadn't noticed the guns. Dylan was deathly afraid of heights. He had turned pale as he approached the plane and terrified as he boarded, but she was wrapped in her own worry to notice.

The flight attendant in her kindest voice bent to him and rubbed his head. "Well, you're in luck. You see, this isn't a plane. It's a jet... a very good jet. And I promise you that you sail through the sky without ever knowing that you left the ground. In fact, we'll put on a fun movie for you. I'll pop you some popcorn."

Winking at Lilly, who smiled back at her gratefully, the flight attendant went to the back of the plane and brought back a snow white bear that Dmitry's daughter Anya played with often.

"Thank you," Dylan said, taking the bear. He rubbed his fluffy fur and eased his shoulders.

It was funny what a simple toy could do to change a child's disposition.

"His name is Goober," the woman said. "I'm sure that his former owner would like for you to have him."

"Really?" he asked, eyes lighting up.

"Absolutely," she said, rubbing through his curly locks.

"Thank you," Lilly mouthed as she eyed Vasily.

He came onto the plane with a small black bag that he sat behind the cockpit door, and then took a seat in the chair facing them. Putting on his seat belt, he motioned for the attendant. "Take us home," he said, looking at Dylan. He noticed in his hand, he was holding Anya's bear.

The woman nodded and went to tell the pilot where their final destination would be.

Finally alone and out of harm's way, Vasily was able to focus on the two people in front of him. Shifting uncomfortably in his seat, he spread his long muscular legs apart and placed his elbows on his knees.

Lilly looked over at him with an intense glare, one arm draped over her son, waiting for him to say something.

Unfortunately, for Vasily, he didn't know what to say. He was a man of very few words and used to keeping all of his emotions, both good and bad, to himself.

"What's your name again?" Dylan finally asked, breaking the thick layer of proverbial ice.

"Vasily," he answered slowly enough for the boy to understand it.

"And you are my mother's friend?" Dylan continued to probe as he held the bear tightly.

Vasily tightened his knitted fingers together. "I am." He looked at Lilly again. "He's very handsome." His wonderment was endless. He'd never seen that particular color of green eyes before, and he had traveled the world. He was fascinated by his little raspy voice and his obvious protective instinct over his mother.

"Thank you. I'd like to think so," she said proudly. "He's an honor student too, very smart."

"Really?" Vasily began to relax as the jet taxied down the tarmac.

"Mr. Vasily?" Dylan said, lifting his chin. His eyes sparkled.

"Please, just Vasily," he answered. "I don't like formalities."

"Why does everyone carry guns on this jet?" Dylan asked innocently.

Vasily smiled and tugged at his suit jacket. *The boy was very observant.* "Well, we all work in security," he said, trying to avoid a lie. "We are like police officers. In order to do our job, we need certain types of equipment." He moved his jacket for Dylan to see. "Carrying the gun is just part of the job. But don't worry, you are completely safe."

The answer seemed to sate Dylan's growing curiosity.

"Where are we going?" Lilly asked.

"Somewhere safe," Vasily answered. "I'd rather not say in front of the... Dylan."

Lilly twisted up her lip. *Did he really expect her to wait until they arrived at where they were going for her to find out?* "*Nu, skazhite mne na russkom yazyke,*" she finally said, crossing her shapely legs.

The small motion caught Vasily's attention, but he tried hard not to outright show his attraction. It was not fitting in this situation, and it might make them both way too uncomfortable, even for such a short flight.

"What did you just say, Mom?" Dylan asked. He had never heard his mother speak in Russian before.

"Doesn't matter, Vasily understood me. That's all that is important."

"*YA otvezu tebya v Memfise , v bezopasnoye mesto,* " he answered, explaining that he was taking her to a safe place in Memphis.

Vasily forgot that she spoke fluent Russian, but was glad that they had some barriers between themselves and the small child. Surely things would come up very soon that would need to be addressed in his presence without him understanding.

As the jet started to taxi down the runway, Dylan's attention quickly shifted from his new fascination with his mother's hidden language skills and Vasily's gun to the uneasy feeling of moving at a rapid speed.

"Mommy," he said, fists balled up.

"It will be okay, honey," she promised.

But Dylan's fear eroded all hopes of him staying calm. Tears forming at the sides of his eyes, he quickly began to turn pale.

Vasily knew that he was supposed to stay in his seat, but he'd also made a million flights around the world both alone and for his boss on this very jet. Unhooking himself, he moved over to Dylan, unlatched his seatbelt and picked him up. Against the pressure of the plane ascending, he sat back down and locked Dylan into the seat with him. Holding him close, he smiled.

"There, is that better?" Vasily asked, wiping Dylan's tears.

Dylan nodded, holding the bear in a choke-hold, and put his head against the man's chest.

Vasily could feel his body heat, feel his heartbeat in his hands and smell the scent of innocence all about him. It was a surreal experience. This human being that he was cradling, this child who was so smart and so beautiful, was his.

He looked over at Lilly, who had stopped breathing all together at the sight of them and noticed the tears in her eyes.

"It will be okay," he said aloud for both Dylan and Lilly. "I'll keep you safe."

She stared at him, tears flowing down her cheeks, hands clutching the armrests and tried to swallow down her sobs. Trembling, she looked over at the flight attendant as she came out of the cockpit once the jet leveled out. "I'll take a double scotch straight up if you have it," she   managed   to   bite   out

Chapter 5

On the far side of the mansion, in his own private wing, the man of the house was far less stressed than his subordinates. After a late dinner with the family and putting his children to sleep in their quarters, he made his way to his master bedroom, an almost vulgarly large space, decorated by the premier designer of the Western hemisphere and overseen by his better half.

When Dmitry and his wife had decided to come back to the States for a while, she had redone the entire mansion to suit them, but spent an extra amount of care on their wing, which was easily 3,000 square feet for four rooms. It was a hideaway from the world with every amenity possible, a place where he could take off his many hats and focusing on the sole job of being a husband.

In the custom-made king sized bed made for his exceptionally long body, Dmitry laid his head comfortably in his wife's lap watching the 90 inch television across the room while she rubbed through his golden locks. He stroked her arm gently and began to doze off when there was a knock on the door.

"Papa," Anatoly said, waiting for his father to answer.

Dmitry looked at the door and then at the clock. With a huff, he rose up, muscles tensing in his six-pack of an abdomen and stretched. "I'll be out in a minute," he said, throwing the sheets off his legs. "What does that boy want now?"

His wife, Royal, rested back in the bed, her statuesque naked body giving off a silhouette in the dimly lit room. Flashing lusty eyes at him, she arched her back and propped up her head on her hands.

"It better be important," she taunted.

"Sorry, sweetheart," he said, pulling himself to the end of the bed and grabbing his pajama bottoms from the nightstand. "I promise if it's not, you're going to lose your only stepson tonight." Quickly slipping on his pants, one leg at a time, he walked to the door and opened it slightly, just enough to look down at his son.

Anatoly didn't wait for him to speak. He knew that he was interrupting. "Vasily's headed here with the woman."

Dmitry didn't like the sound of that. "Why here?"

"Get this. He got there to swoop her up and take her somewhere and found out she had his kid."

"He has a child?" Dmitry thought Vasily hardly seemed the type.

"He didn't know," Anatoly said, tilting his head. "Sound familiar?"

Dmitry scratched the blonde stubble growing on his neck. "Very." He looked back at his wife and felt a stir. She lay across the bed, black hair fanned across the pillow waiting for him. "Let me know when he gets here. Text me and I'll come down so that we can talk briefly."

Anatoly knew that answer. His father had plans of rolling around in the sack with his wife all night, and didn't want to be bothered. "Should I just call for you in the morning?" he asked.

Dmitry debated. He really didn't want to be disturbed anymore tonight, but he'd learned that procrastination could cost lives. He leaned up against the door frame and huffed. "I would say yes, but considering the nature of their visit, we should discuss all of the specifics tonight."

Anatoly winked at his father. "A simple no would have sufficed, Papa." Tapping the door lightly with his knuckles, he called out to his stepmother. "Sorry to bother you, Royal."

"No you're not," Royal called out with a laugh from the bed. "Go away. Go be with your wife," she ordered.

Dmitry smiled at her, loving her sense of humor. "She's right, you know. You've been up working long enough. Go enjoy yourself. A hard day's work deserves a hard night's play."

Anatoly rolled his eyes. *Was his father really trying to give him sex advice on top of everything else?* "Papa, Renee and I aren't as old as you two... well, *as old as you*. We can have sex more than at night."

Dmitry winked at him. "It's not about quantity; its quality." Closing the door behind him, he turned and looked at Royal. "You ready for your nap cap, my love?" he asked, pulling his pants off and throwing them across the room.

"Starving for it," she giggled.

***

From the moment that the jet landed in Memphis, Lilly saw that the man that she had once known was no more. He was no longer just a foot soldier, no longer just a nameless face in a small crew of street gangsters or a low-level Russian mobster. He'd climbed the ranks.

He was met by 10 men in three Yukon Denali trucks on the tarmac. All of them regarded him with more respect than she'd ever seen Leo's men treat him with and none of them seemed lowly.

She and Dylan were quickly taken to a truck, separate from Vasily and then driven straight to the compound.

As the large iron gates opened and the guards waved them through, she couldn't help but sit up and marvel at the mansion in the distance, illuminated by lights on the lawn and crawling with bodyguards, big guns and dogs. She had never seen anything like it up close. It was something out of Gone with the Wind with plantation-style white pillars and columns, but the size of it and the design spoke to an architectural interpretation of the old south with a much more modern twist.

"Excuse me. Whose house is this?" she asked.

The man looked at her through the rear-view mirror, but said nothing.

When the truck stopped up front, Vasily opened the door for her as another bodyguard opened Dylan's door and picked him up. He was still clutching the bear, even in his sleep.

"Let's get you inside," Vasily said, offering his large hand.

She took it and stepped out. Her heart pounded in her chest, nervousness causing the small ball in her stomach to tighten. At that moment, she was more afraid than Dylan had been on the plane.

"Where are we?" She nervously licked her dry lips. "Is this your home?"

He chuckled. "No," he said, shaking his head. "We're at my boss's house."

"Well, who in the hell is your boss with a place like this?" she asked.

As they approached the elaborate front entry of solid mahogany double doors with forged iron, a butler in a black suit opened them and stepped aside quietly.

Everyone was in a damned suit, even well after midnight, she thought to herself. Suddenly, she felt extremely underdressed, like maybe she should have been going through the side door or the back door.

"This is the Medlov compound," he said, feeling her jerk away as he crossed the threshold. He turned to her, looked down at her visibly afraid and rubbed her face. "You are safe, Lilly. I promise."

Her eyes told on her. Even only briefly as Leo's wife, she had heard of Dmitry Medlov in whispered conversations. He was a legend. In fact, she hardly believed him to be real, because the stories were so wild.

She saw the bodyguard holding her son in his arms headed through the foyer.

"Where is he taking him?" she asked, forgetting her fear. She bolted toward him.

"Let him rest," Vasily urged, grabbing her arm gently. "They are taking him to the east wing. Once you and I have a conversation with my boss, then you'll be escorted there and that is where you'll stay until we get this all sorted out."

The butler closed the doors behind her and made her jump.

"Sorry," she apologized.

"Lilly, there really is no reason for you to worry. No one here will hurt you."

The words resonated with Lilly. *Hurt her. Worry.* Whether she liked it or not, that was her world. And it wasn't until that very moment, hearing those very words, that she realized that she was tired of running, tired of being tortured by the idea of Leo finding her.

Running a hand over her chest, she took a deep breath and shook her head. "Do you realize how hard this is, Vasily? This afternoon, I was in Jackson, Mississippi in my own broke down, country home, cooking bologna and cheese sandwiches for lunch and watching Disney with my son because I can't afford the swanky channels like HBO. I have less than a thousand bucks in cash, and it's all in a coffee can in my $4 Salvation Army purse... all because I can't put my real name on a bank account. Tonight, I'm inside of a multi-million dollar paramilitary compound of one of the most feared Russian mafia leaders in the *world*. So when you tell me that I have no reason to worry, I know that's a lie. I have every reason to worry." She pursed her lips together and wiped a tear. "And I'm scared shitless, man."

The men standing in the foyer around Vasily quickly dispersed. They knew when to exit, and it was obvious that their boss needed his privacy.

Silently, Vasily stood staring at her until everyone was gone. He slowly walked up to her. Their proximity caused electricity to erupt between them.

She looked up into his eyes with want and need like he'd never seen a woman look at him before.

"Come here," he said, taking her trembling hand in his.

Wrapping his arms around her, he gave her a warm hug. His heat engulfed her and his smell intoxicated her, his muscles insulated her and for a moment, just a moment, she felt safe.

A throat cleared behind them, and suddenly Vasily went rigid. Releasing her, he turned around quickly.

"Boss," he said, straightening his suit.

Anatoly looked at Lilly and a fair brow shot up. "The plot thickens," he said, walking up to Vasily. "I always pegged you as the traditional type."

Lilly's eyes narrowed. *Was he a racist? Was that a racist remark?*

"A man has his secrets," Vasily said under his breath.

"I'm Anatoly Medlov," Anatoly said, offering his hand to Lilly. "Welcome to our humble abode."

"I'm Lilly," she answered carefully. "Thank you for having me."

To provoke him would surely be a bad idea. This strange man with his famous last name was younger than Vasily by some years and also incredibly handsome. Most of the men of the Vory v Zakone that she had known all had a very distinct eastern bloc look to them, but Vasily and Leo and now Anatoly were much different.

They were all unusually handsome, dangerous and very rich.

Anatoly was dressed in dark jeans, a black t-
shirt that fit his muscular arms and black boots.
His curly mop of blonde curls was magnified by
crystal blue eyes and a wide, pink mouth. He
was overtly gorgeous, but his eyes were dark
and brooding.

There was no softness in them, leading her
to believe that despite his relaxed demeanor at
the moment, he could be quite difficult to
manage if he were angry.

Anatoly looked around the foyer and
shrugged. "Where's the kid?"

"I had him sent to the east wing," Vasily answered. "He was pretty worn out after the
trip."

"Damn, I wanted to see who he favored,"
Anatoly said, looking at Lilly. "Why don't you
just tell me? I'll see him later."

"His name is Dylan," Lilly answered, know-
ing what Anatoly underlying questions was.
"And he looks like his father." She looked up at
Vasily.

"Well, that's an answer," Anatoly said sarcastically as he looked at his watch. *Not the*

confirmation that he was hoping for, but he wouldn't push it if Vasily didn't. "Papa wants to meet us in his study. I recommend that we beat him there and grab a drink before he arrives. There will be questions, followed by directives, followed by one of his glorious speeches. And I'm fucking exhausted. So let's get this show on the road." He turned on his heels and headed into the main hall of the house.

Vasily nodded. "Let's go," he told Lilly. "We don't want to keep Boss Medlov waiting."

Which one, she said to herself, as she followed the two men.

Chapter 6

The palatial Medlov mansion was a thing of absolute beauty. Never had Lilly seen such breathtaking chandeliers, vibrant and expensive paintings, large exotic flower arrangements, exquisite furniture pieces and extravagant ceilings and flooring in her entire life. She took in her surroundings as best she could. But the mansion was so massive, so very luxurious that it was hard to fathom that one family lived here.

Every room that she passed, she tried to spy a quick look, but following the men who led her made the simple task that much harder. Their strides were long and powerful, and they all moved with unwavering purpose. She almost felt as though she was running through the hall or at least moving a jogger's speed to keep up.

Nearly every 50 feet down the long corridor she saw a guard, dressed in the same type of black suit, tactical gear or jeans. They all had tattoos and accents, and a look of clear loyalty and devotion. *That was normal in a situation like this*. But what was odd, unique, was the way that all of the men interacted with each other. This was their home, their place in the world. They all seemed to regard it as such and as a result, she imagined, they took on a role of protector that meant a great deal more than just someone who was paid to do a job.

Her heart pounded in her chest as she sat on the brown leather sofa in the elaborately designed and extremely masculine study – a room big enough to fit over half of her home.

Anatoly poured each of them a glass of vodka at the bar in the far corner of the room, while Vasily reviewed all the monitors on the other wall, leaving her to her thoughts.

Did Vasily think that she looked pretty anymore without all the diamonds, designer clothes and expensive hair weaves? Did he think that she looked dramatically older or heavier? She had picked up a few pounds since the baby. No doubt that he was surrounded by beautiful women now, many of them vying for his complete attention.

She berated herself quietly for even caring as long as he kept her safe, but she couldn't help it. She wanted him to see her, but more than that, she wanted him to feel the same thing that she felt for him.

Pulling her hair back behind her ear, she tried to catch a glimpse of herself in the over-sized mirror across the room without being too obvious. When she saw herself, she instantly wished that she hadn't. She didn't have on a smudge of lipstick from biting at her lips in nervousness. Her eyeliner was smudged from crying, and she was sure that she needed a bath.

Sheesh, tonight couldn't be worse.

In all the uproar back in Mississippi, she had forgotten to freshen up. At that moment, it was life and death, but now that she was at least a little safer, reality was starting to creep in.

It was too late to fix up and cover up. He'd seen her at her worse.

He probably thinks I'm some charity case, she thought to herself. The idea of such a thing tugged at the strings of her once-fortified pride. Sure, she didn't have money, but before tonight, she still had her pride intact.

Anatoly walked over to where she was sitting on the leather sofa and passed her one of the three tumblers gripped between his fingers. "Do you like vodka?" he asked. "Sorry, I didn't ask before I began to pour."

"Sure," she said, taking the glass. Before he could turn around, she downed the contents and hissed. "Can I have another?" she asked, bucking her eyes at the burn.

Anatoly smirked and turned back to her and gave her another glass. "Rough night?"

"The roughest," she replied sincerely. "I haven't had this much to drink in years."

"Well, this situation definitely qualifies as stressful," Anatoly said, looking at his watch.

The closed door flung open and a guard came in followed by Dmitry, now dressed in a pair of jeans and t-shirt. As he walked in, Vasily stood up from his chair and went rigid. Lilly, on the other hand, wasn't sure what to do. Should she stand? *Shit*, should she kneel? *Who was this guy?*

Dmitry walked over to her and offered a hand. "Hello," he said with a warm smile. "You must be Vasily's Lilly."

Lilly *was* beyond shocked. This mountain of a man was Dmitry Medlov? His inhuman perfection was almost vulgar. Not only was he tall, muscular and tan, but also blonde and handsome, he had an air about him that made her feel that he was truly royalty of some sort.

She couldn't help but smile. Placing her small hand in his, she shook it back. "I am," she said, proud of the title, *Vasily's Lilly.*

"Well, it's very nice to meet you. I'm just so sorry that it had to be under these circumstances." He motioned back at the sofa. "Please sit back down. Try to relax. I'm sure that you must be exhausted both mentally and physically."

Dmitry's demeanor made the tension ease a bit. She was expecting a monster, but the man standing before her was hardly that. "I just appreciate everything. I can't say it enough," she said, sitting back down.

"Well, as soon as Vasily heard, he headed straight toward you," Dmitry said, walking over to the front of his desk. He leaned against it and crossed his arms across his chest. "But I was also told of a little surprise once he got there." He looked over at Vasily, who had made his way closer to Lilly during the introductions.

"Yes," Lilly said, looking over at Vasily. "My son." She instantly corrected herself. *Force of habit.* Shaking her head, she tried it again. "Our son."

Dmitry looked in between the both of them. "Well, which is it?"

Vasily was behind the sofa, standing directly above Lilly. Putting a hand on her shoulder, he spoke up. "He's mine. I can vouch for her. I've seen him. He's my boy."

"No disrespect to you, Lilly, but are we sure about this?" Dmitry asked carefully.

"Certain," Lilly answered.

Behind her without words, Vasily nodded.

The confirmation was just what he wanted to hear. Dmitry nodded. "Well, we've all been there. Let me be the first to congratulate you, Vasily." Clasping his hands together, he yawned and shook his head, fighting sleep after a sex session from hell with his wife. "So, Lilly, you'll be staying with us for a while, at least until we get this business with Leo Rasputin under control. As I understand it, we are not really sure if he is looking for you or not.

So, we've got some feelers out there to get an idea of what he's looking for. If it's not you, then well, you can go on with your life. If it is you, then that's why we are here."

She felt herself bristle at the thought. "I hope that we're all just over reacting."

Dmitry smiled at her. "But you don't think that we are, do you?"

She nodded no.

"Why do you think that?" Dmitry asked.

"Because I know Leo," she said voice shaky. "He wants revenge for me testifying against him. I put him in jail."

"And you did that why?" Dmitry probed further. He needed to see where the woman's head was to make sure that they were making the right decision.

Lilly swallowed hard. "I had to get back at him for what he'd done to Vasily. He shot him, almost killed him, just for trying to protect me. I had to get him back for all the beatings I took. I had to get him back for all the times he had caused me pure and utter humiliation."

Dmitry hated the idea of a man beating on a woman. He looked at her now, obviously fighting for what little life she had been able to make for herself and felt sorry for her. "Well, the Medlov Men are not saints. I don't want to give you that appearance. It would be a false one. But we don't beat women. However, I have to be honest with you and tell you that that is not the reason that you are here."

Lilly looked up confused. Why was she here then?

Dmitry looked up at Vasily. "If I housed every beaten, bitter ex-wife or ex-girlfriend of one of my men, then I'd have a house full and a lot of bad relationships with families across the world. You are here, because Vasily is family and you are the mother of his child." He wanted to make himself perfectly clear. "That said I expect you to be completely honest with me."

"I have been," she answered sincerely.

"Does Leo Rasputin have any other reason to look for you?" Dmitry asked. "Is this search driven by more than just revenge? I have to be honest; it sounds like it's about money." He looked up at Vasily.

"It could only be about revenge," Lilly answered. "I don't have anything else."

Dmitry hated to ask in front of Vasily but he had to know. "And are you still married to him?"

He looked over at her curiously. He had never thought about that? Was she still married to him?

"No. I filed for divorce during the time that he was detained by the FBI," she answered. "It was finalized while he was in prison."

Dmitry knew that there would be a far greater push back from the other Russian mafia families if she were still his wife. "Good," he said, more confident in his decision to help.

Quietly Vasily exhaled a sigh of relief. He knew the law and if Lilly was still married, then that made Dylan his son legally, and that he simply could not take.

Dmitry nodded and stood up. He had heard everything that he needed to know directly from the source. "Find out what Leo wants," he said to Vasily and Anatoly. "And make this quick."

"I will," Vasily said stepping from behind the sofa as Dmitry passed.

Dmitry looked between Vasily and Lilly and smiled. "It looks like to me that everyone here needs to get some rest. So, please go to your quarters and do just that."

As quickly as he was there, Dmitry was gone. He and his men disappeared back out of the door and down the hall, leaving the original three alone in the study.

Anatoly rolled his neck and picked up the bottle of vodka he had been pouring from earlier. *Now, it really was time for him to call it quits.* Yawning, he walked toward the door. "I'm taking this upstairs to my wife and run her a hot bath, *if she isn't already asleep.* You two have a good night. We'll see you in the morning. Lilly, I'm sure that Vasily will give you a rundown of the grounds and what to do and what not to do. So, I'll leave you in his very capable hands. It was nice to meet you."

"You too," Lilly said, glad to finally be alone with Vasily again.

As the door closed, she deflated. Turning toward him, she ran a hand through her hair. "Wow," she whispered. Words were too difficult at the moment. She just needed to let it all settle into her head. After all that she had seen, and all that she had been through.

Vasily saw her visibly grappling with everything and took her hand. "I'll take you to your room."

Lilly wiped a tear from her eye. "Is my son in the room with me? I'd really feel more comfortable if he were. I don't want to impose..."

Vasily cut her off. "He's in the room with you, and you're not imposing on anyone. Once you've had a chance to rest, you'll be able to think clearer," he assured her, rubbing her back gently.

She looked up at him, thankful for his tempered strength. *God, bless him. He was trying.* "Okay, well take me to my temporary home."

"Come with me," he said, motioning toward the door.

As Lilly and Vasily walked through the house, alone and slow this time, Vasily gave her a tour. Each room had a story, one that either he had been there for or heard about. Relaxed and composed, he told her funny stories about his time with Anatoly and Dmitry and how much he had learned under their leadership.

"I can tell that you've grown," she said to him as they made their way up the back staircase.

"Time here has given me clarity," he confessed.

"Can I ask a question completely off of subject here?" Getting to the top of the staircase, she looked around the second floor now in just sheer amazement. "How big is this place?"

He looked up at the ceiling to recall. "17,000 square feet," he said, guiding her down the dimly lit corridor.

"17... " Lilly shook her head. "You need a map to get around this house."

"You learn it over time, but at first, it can be intimidating," he said with a shrug. "So, what is your question?" he asked, stopping and turning toward her.

"That *was* my question," Lilly said with a laugh. "How big is this freaking house?"

Vasily also laughed. As he did, his face lit up and Lilly couldn't help but stop and look at him. *Wow, he was still so incredibly handsome*. It made her heart skip a beat just to see him happy, to see some glimmer of something other than gloom. "It's really good to see you smile," she said, voice wispy. "I don't think that I've seen that in a very long time." Her head ducked shyly. "It suits you."

He tilted his head. *Was that a compliment?* "It's just good to see you, period." He stepped closer.

The smile left Lilly's face. It was inevitable that they would arrive back at the conversation about *the elephant in the room*. She was just relieved that they were alone.

Licking her dry lips, she beetled her thick black brows at him. "You may not believe this, but I wanted to tell you, Vasily," she said, heart beating faster by the second.

She could see it in his face. He needed to hear her say it. He needed a real explanation, though he was respectful enough not to demand one at the time.

Despite her nervousness, Lilly kept her voice pitched low and even. "I didn't know until after you were gone that I was pregnant. *Six weeks after to be exact*. And after everything that we'd gone through both together and apart, I thought the only way to keep us *all* safe was to keep my secret." Huge raindrop like tears began to form again, but she tried to fight them. "Giving birth in a hospital for the poor wasn't exactly my dream way of bringing a kid into the world, you know." Her mouth began to quiver. As she blinked over and over, the tears fell to her cheeks. "But after I saw him for the first time on the ultrasound all small and perfect, there was no way that I was going to get rid of him." She huffed. "But then reality set in. If I called you, if I said anything, then maybe the word would have gotten out and I would have put him in danger. And I know you, albeit not very well, I know you well enough to know that you would have done anything for us. But what you hadn't considered is that I'd do anything for you too."

Vasily was quiet, deathly still. His face was stoic, hiding every emotion that he felt or wanted to feel, but she could see it in his stance. He was without a doubt relieved to know that she still felt something for him.

"You don't have to explain your decision to keep Dylan to me," he said softly. "I just wish that I could have had an active role in his life. A boy needs a father."

"What about what you said in the car?" she asked confused.

He frowned. "What did I say in the car?"

"You asked me why I had done this to you?" she said, astonished that he had already forgotten such a cruel insult.

"I meant, *why did you keep him from me*?" He looked away. "I may not be the best person, I'll admit that, but I'm not the worst." Inwardly, he wasn't sure about that, even as he said it, considering his profession.

Lilly exhaled a deep breath. "Wow," she said, shaking her head. "I thought you meant something else." Her eyes watered again. "I thought you meant… "

"No," Vasily said, cutting her off. *He didn't want to hear what she had thought he meant.* He knew what he had meant and that was enough.

"That's a major relief." Wiping a tear from her eye, she laughed. "I am an emotional wreck today, huh? I mean, look at me. I'm a mess." She sniffled and wiped her nose. "And I think I stink."

A laugh escaped him again. "You don't stink," he said with a grin.

Vasily watched her with unadulterated fascination. Lilly was both soft and commanding in her presence. She was so strong, stronger than he had ever expected. Yet, she seemed not to know it. *So self-conscious.* "You're... beautiful," he said in a matter-of-fact tone. "More beautiful than I ever remembered." Wiping her cheek with his thumb, he paused, wanting very much to kiss her heart-shaped lips, wanting very much to do so many things.

She looked up at him, waiting for his next move, breathing hard, eyes wide.

The tension in the hallway reached fever pitch, both realizing at the same time that while time had passed, their attraction to each other had not. In fact, it might have grown.

After some insidious thought that made him curl up his bottom lip, Vasily finally relaxed his shoulders. "Let me take you to your room," he said, stepping back.

Lilly exhaled reluctantly. Some things had remained the absolute same no matter how many years passed. Vasily had always been a hard man to understand. Often, one would never know what he was thinking until acted on it.

She guessed tonight would be no different in that regard.

Walking with him down the dimly lit hall side-by-side, she pushed back all the things that she wanted to say to him. When they got to her bedroom door, she simply bit out, "Thank you for everything." Her heart was still trying to leap up into her throat. "I know that I've said it a hundred times, but... "

Vasily cut her off. "You don't have to thank me." *For one thing, it made him uncomfortable.* He looked away. "If you need anything, I'll be right next door." He pointed at the door several feet down the hall to a door that they had already passed. "That's my room."

"I would say the same thing here, but it's pretty clear that you can't read signs," she said, winking at him. She wanted to plant a seed, to let him know in some way it was okay to speak in more than three sentences at a time to her.

Vasily was speechless. Pursing his lips together, he narrowed his gaze on her.

"Have a good night," she said, going into her room and shutting the door.

Chapter 7

Vasily peeled out of his suit, one slow layer at a time and threw it over in the corner of his large bedroom on the leather sofa for the maid to pick up and clean the next day. Like every night before, he put his designer shoes in the walk-in closet, lined up perfectly with his other shoes. Took off his platinum watch and placed it in the jewelry tray with his clip of $100 bills and his wallet, along with his Saint Jude cross necklace. Carefully, he laid his guns on his dresser across from his very inviting bed, and looked at himself in the mirror, shirtless and covered in tattoos.

He almost didn't recognize himself tonight.

Running a hand over the scar on his chest where Leo had shot him, he slipped into a daze.

Over and over in his mind, he played out the entire day, remembering each and every single detail. Lilly's lips. Her eyes. Dylan's smile. His hair. Her smell. His voice.

He swam in a sea of new sensations, head barely above water, and tried to make sense of it all.

The reality was that when he woke up this morning, he was just Vasily. No family. No children. No ties. A true Vor; living by the code of the great men before him.

Tonight, however, he had an entire ready-made family in the next bedroom, depending on him for everything from food, clothes and shelter to safety from a very vengeful crime lord.

What were the odds?

One thing was for sure, he'd never cast another judging thought toward his bosses for getting married and having children. Before he had secretly harbored a little frustration against them for complicating their situations by creating families, especially considering what the risks would always be. Now, he understood at least half of the equation.

Seeing Lilly tonight, after all those years, felt like someone stuck his head through an electric current. He wasn't surprised that the last thing that she'd done before going to her bedroom was to challenge him. It seemed that her entire purpose in his life had been to do just that, even when she didn't mean to. What did surprise him was the fact that he had done nothing about it.

He wasn't a saint.

He had been with more than his fair share of women.

So, why hadn't he told her how he truly felt?

Maybe it was that he felt she was too vulnerable right now to make some cheap pass on her.

Maybe it was the fact that she was the mother of his child.

Maybe it was nerves.

He slammed his hand down on the dresser and shook his head. *Damn that woman.* She was going to drive him crazy. Trying to get his bearings, he bent over and ran his hand over his buzzed crew cut and shook his head.

It had been so long since he had had her. So long since he had held her in his arms, tasted her sweet plush lips, felt her soft brown skin against his and her heart beat against his chest. It was a torturous fact, but he still remembered her face when he was in between her thighs, how her mouth parted as he entered her. How she closed around him and took him into her velvety folds and made him forget everything and everyone.

Seeing her again, brought the desire back that he had before, he'd been able to control, *damn near ignore*. But after he had seen her, after he had fallen for her even without touching her, out of necessity, he had to avoid her just to keep the glimmer of hope from being exposed in some unplanned moment between them.

The truth of the matter was that 10 years ago, when he ran up the stairs of Leo's home to save her and was shot as a reward for his trouble, the pain didn't come from the sneaky bullet of the hidden body guard, but her ultimate rejection of him by her. He wanted to die on that cold, wooden floor after she had recoiled away from what he offered. *Protection. Respect. A new beginning.*

When he had recovered from his wounds, all he had felt was a fog of fury.

But when Yakov contacted him nearly a year later and told him what she had done – testified against her husband just to seek revenge for that night – he had known that whatever deep emotion had drawn him to her, she had felt also. Perhaps, just as strongly, but no doubt enough to break the chains that Leo held on her.

And now she was here.

Next door.

"What the fuck am I doing?" He mumbled as he rose up from his slumped position. He couldn't let her slip out of his fingers again, just to protect some foolish pride.

Heading quickly, in just his boxers, back out of his bedroom, he stalked down the hall to her door and raised his hand to knock on it.

Check the knob, something told him as he lowered his hand before he could disturb her or worse, wake up Dylan.

He twisted it open and stepped inside as quietly as possible.

Dylan was asleep under the heavy duvet covers in the large, elevated queen-sized canopy bed, snoring lightly and completely oblivious to the world around him.

Proud, Vasily fought a smirk. *No one could conquer that bed. It was legendary.* Walking as softly as he could over to the bed, he pulled the covers up on Dylan's little body and bent to kiss his curly mop of hair.

The boy smelled of sticky sweets and his mother's perfume, just like a child should.

And then as if to completely smitten Vasily, the boy smiled in his sleep.

So innocent, Vasily thought to himself as he stood over his son. He aimed to keep him that way for as long as this world would let him. At that moment, he realized that he had a new purpose in life and it was not only to serve the Medlov family, which he would always do, but also to serve this young child.

He stood there in silence, committing everything he could about the boy to memory. Assailed with visions Dylan growing older, he felt himself warming up from the inside out. Hope began to sneak into empty places like water filling a pot of dry soil. He felt himself renewed, bursting with new energy.

The draw to Lilly was unexpectedly intensified.

He could hear the water shooting out of the shower head in the adjoining bathroom and the echo of it as it hit a body instead of the marble floor. Moving quietly from the boy, he went to her.

Evidently, she really did think that she stunk. He hadn't left her, in his mind, long enough for her to have jumped in the shower, but a woman on a mission couldn't be stopped.

She had her body facing away from the door, leaning against the cool marble wall, allowing the sheets of hot water to cover her from head to feet. At that angle, it was impossible for her to know that she was no longer alone. He closed the bathroom door behind them quietly and pulled down his black boxers. Fully naked, manhood growing with every step, he walked over to the shower.

He appraised her with needy eyes, soaking in her feature. Her body was shapelier now that she'd had a child. Her back was thick with muscle probably from carrying her son and doing manual labor. She still boasted an incredibly thin waist, wide hips, a curvaceous bottom worthy of being kissed, runner's legs, thick calves and small gold anklet on her left leg. Her natural hair curled up against her back and her shoulders, glistening with water.

Resting on her elbows, she rolled her neck and looked up at the showerhead for the water to splash in her face.

He couldn't watch a moment longer. Opening the door to the shower, he startled her. She turned; brown bobbing breasts exposed and sucked in a gasp. The look on her face told him that she'd wanted him to come to her, even though she wasn't sure that he would.

Control and domination shaded his masculine features as he stepped inside the shower with her. "Did I read your signs correctly this time?" Vasily asked, walking up to her in the water.

Lilly was speechless. Stuttering, she wiped the water from her eyes and tried to avert her eyes from his engorged member and carved abs to his handsome face. "I meant for you to kiss me," she said, breaths dragging.

He pulled her by her waist to him, forcing her to feel his bare skin against her own. "What makes you think that I won't kiss you?"

Lilly was praying that he would.

Picking her up off the ground, he made her wrap her legs around him. With one hand on her back and the other under her bottom, muscles bulging, manhood erect, he laid a gentle, teasing kiss on her parted mouth, sucking on her lips and then her tongue, going deeper and deeper with each revolution. The silkiness of the kiss was sweet. She felt his breaths as he taste her. Sucking him in, she wrapped her legs tighter, unable to get close enough to him.

She gasped as the water poured over them, but kissed him back as eagerly as he had kissed her. "I've missed you," was all she could get out before he pinned her up against the wall.

He paused and looked at her, trying to decide what to kiss first. His eyes were blazing with fire, saying all the things that his mouth would not.

Even though the water consumed them, heat exploded.

With her arms wrapped around him, she pulled him in closer to her hardening nipples. He ran another sweet kiss from her lips, down her long neck to her aching breasts. Suckling her rigid nipples and fondling her with his tongue, he looked up into her eyes as he hoisted her up to watch her eyes roll to the back of her head.

Her sex was swelling now, barely an inch from his throbbing penis. He ached to be inside of her, ached to fill her tighten around him again.

"Are you on birth control?" he asked, gripping her back.

"Mirena," she whispered.

"What's that?" His eyes flashed open.

"Birth control," she answered, holding him tighter. "Are you safe?" *God, please let him be safe*, she thought to herself.

"Yes," he sputtered in between kisses all over her body. "But it's been a while."

"For me too. You have no idea," she whimpered. "But please, Vasily, be careful with me." Her tone was full of warning.

He grabbed her chin and made her look at him. "Lilly, I would never hurt you."

As he said the words, all fear evaporated.

She bent to kiss his sculpted, sensual lips again. This time sucking on his bottom lip harder.

Her legs parted further, and she found his head at the apex of her blossoming flower. It had been so long until she could feel herself on the verge of eruption at just the thought of him being inside of her. His roaming hands only made it worse. He massaged her swollen sex, bringing milk down in a pool between her legs, catching her clit in between his index and middle finger and using his knuckles to arouse her to the point of madness.

His luminescent eyes were fixed on her, water splashing over his perfectly tanned skin and giving all the more allure to his carved, intense build.

She ran her hand over the scar on his chest and looked up at him in shame and pity. He would never know what a burden she had carried all these years knowing that he would have never gone through any of it, if he had simply not loved her.

"I'm still so sorry, Vasily," she whispered.

Speaking into her mouth, he said softly, "You don't have to ever apologize again."

He put his hand over her lips, refusing to hear her heartfelt apology, as he eased her down and parted her body. The erotic connection caused a chain reaction. Her head flung back as she undulated on top of him, rotating her hips to feel the full circumference of his unforgiving enormity. Her lips parted, eyes rolled again and back arched.

The sight of her being pleased was hypnotic for Vasily. The way she moved. The way she felt. *Damn it*! He guided her carefully, slowly, only going an inch at a time until he was buried to the hilt inside of her.

They both let out an audible sigh of ecstasy as he held her up without effort and began to pump inside of her. His hips moved at a rhythmic pace, slow, circular, intentional thrusts that began a literal paradigm shift in their realities.

Domineering hunger took over. His thrusts became more powerful, lifting her in the air as he moaned.

"Am I enough for you?" he asked, eyeing her as she lifted her head to look up at the ceiling.

She had forgotten how demanding he was inside of her. How skilled he was at what he did. The water from the shower and the wetness from their body covered them both while he moved her up and down his shaft. The sound of skin slapping against skin drowned out the powerful shower head. In his clutches now, she felt the continual and the deliberate pump inside of her body, against her G-spot, against her pearl.

Her moans became louder. Holding him tight, she moved with him back and forth, up and down, forgetting where she was or who she was. His muscles bulged and felt like steel under skin as she balanced herself. Bucking harder and harder now, on the verge of that sweet earthquake.

He watched her as she rode him against the wall, determined to please her, to satisfy her, to conquer her.

Voice nearly failing, she dug her nails into his back as a commanding climax swept over her body in angry, hard waves.

"Yes!" she called out loudly, body convulsing and paralyzing at the same time. "Oh, Vasily!"

"What, baby. Tell me," he taunted her. Making her look into his eyes, he pumped harder. "Tell me," he demanded in a growl.

"I love you," she said as the wave ended.

Looking into his eyes, she let a tear fall. Breathing hard, she held on to him and said it again as she felt her muscles contracting. "I love you, Vasily."

Chapter 8

Vasily wasn't a late sleeper, but for the first time in years, he actually slept past his internal alarm clock set to wake him up every morning by 5 a.m. It was Lilly's fault, rather her beautiful body that continued to tempt him. They had gone to bed late, making love again as quietly as possible in the bathroom only minutes after they finished the first time.

He just couldn't get enough of her, no matter how hard he tried. Every kiss and touch brought back more memories and more latent desires that had gone unaddressed for too long. He had poured everything that he had into her, which left him drained and confused. Such a thing would have made him feel embarrassed normally, but by the tears in her eyes and the words that she whispered to him, made him know that she felt it also.

After their love making session, they had taken one more shower, void of sex but plenty of kissing. After which, he gave her some of his pajamas and a t-shirt to sleep in; then she finally passed out beside Dylan in the bed.

Unable to leave her, he fell asleep on the small sofa across from her bed, but not before watching her rest for hours by his son. It was such a beautiful and haunting sight until he simply could not look away. To know that they had been out in the world all this time, unattended scared the hell out of him. Yet, to know what he had in his future now was more exciting than any adventure he'd ever known.

For a man his size, the sleep had been rough and hard, but it was worth it to make her feel comfortable her first night in Dmitry's home. Evidently, he had done his job, because once she closed her eyes and snuggled up beside Dylan, she was out like a light.

As his eyes flashed open to the sun a few hours later, he straightened his long body from its crooked position and pulled the throw cover from his legs. As he did, he noticed that he wasn't the only one up.

Dylan sat up in the bed quietly waiting for his mother to rise from her peaceful slumber beside him and reading *Diary of a Wimpy Kid*. Immediately, his eyes lit up when he saw Vasily finally stir across the room. He waved innocently and pointed at his mother to let him know to stay quiet.

Vasily nodded and motioned for him to get out of the bed and meet him at the door. Grabbing Dylan's overnight bag off the side of the bed, he led the little guy out in the hallway and closed the door quietly behind him.

"Mommy's tired. She works long hours at the restaurant," Dylan explained. His raspy little voice sounded too mature for his eight years.

"When a mother loves you, she does what she can," Vasily said, unsure of what else to say to the boy. "You always stand guard over her when she's asleep?"

"Yeah, I try to watch over her. She's the only family that I have." Dylan rubbed his growling stomach. "Mr. Vasily, I'm hungry," Dylan said, looking up at his father.

Vasily's face frowned. "Don't call me that."

"Call you what?" Dylan asked.

"Mister," Vasily rubbed Dylan's mop of curls. His locks were just like that when he was a boy. "Just Vasily will do," he said, walking with him to his room. He opened the door. "I'm right here."

Dylan would adhere to Vasily's wishes but didn't like it. He put up one last protest. "Mom said that children should address all adults as either mister or misses. She says that it's a sign of respect for your elders."

Vasily could appreciate that, but still didn't want to be called by a title. "I'm sure that she'll understand this one exception."

"Where are we going?" Dylan's apprehension rose. Looking through the door, he paused.

Vasily yawned and cracked his back. "Why don't you get dressed in my room, and I'll take you downstairs to grab a bite to eat. Let your mom rest for a while."

"Okay, but I'm not sure if she'll be happy. I'm not supposed to go off with strangers."

Vasily had to chuckle. The kid was already pretty hard around the edges, maybe a good thing for his situation. "She taught you well, but again, I think she'll make an exception."

"Mommy makes a lot of exceptions for you, huh," Dylan asked.

"You have no idea," Vasily said, patting the boy on the back.

They went into the bedroom, but Vasily left the door open just in case Lilly came looking for him, and *just in case he wasn't the exception*.

***

Breakfast in the Medlov compound was not only the most important meal of the day but also one of the few times that everyone got a chance to see each other at one time before they all went about their business.

The staff of five would start to prepare the food way before dawn, making sure that even the earliest riser had coffee, juice and fruit before the full assorted breakfast was served. However, considering they were such a large family comprised of Dmitry, his wife Royal and their three children, Anatoly, his wife Renee and child and Gabriel and his girlfriend Briggy, plus the guards, which Dmitry fed every day, there was plenty of food to prepare.

Still, it was a daily ritual that Dmitry insisted upon and everyone else looked forward to.

By seven in the morning a buffet of food lined the kitchen table, bar and countertops and the informal dining room was set for a family of seven plus three high chairs.

The television in the kitchen was normally on for everyone to watch the news. And following breakfast there was a meeting held by Vasily to go over the directives for security for the day.

Like clockwork, no matter the day, no matter the season, breakfast happened.

Slowly, the families descended from their quarters in the house to the kitchen area, yawning and searching out the smell of freshly brewed Columbian coffee.

Dmitry was always the first to arrive, followed by his wife. The last one to show was always Anatoly, because he had to go to the kennels and feed his dogs; tagging along with him was his shadow, Vasily.

But today was different.

Anatoly went out to the grounds with Boris, a thing that had never happened before, while Vasily slept late.

There was a roar of laughter coming from the dining room as the family sat around the festive table. The smell of pancakes and croissants, rice and gravy, grits and sausage filled the downstairs.

An assortment of hot and cold dishes was presented on the customary fine china. Fresh bouquets of flowers in beautiful crystal vases were placed in the middle of the table and on the buffet and the best silverware had been set out per Royal's instructions after she found out that they would be having a couple of guests.

The windows were opened and curtains pulled to allow the bright sunshine inside, which illuminated the already beautiful interior and set the mood for a great day.

As normal, Dmitry was at the head of the table reading the newspaper with his gold rimmed glasses perched on his perfect nose with Royal to the immediate right of him, using her iPad to check her emails. Gabriel joked with his girlfriend Briggy about her snoring lightly at night while Anatoly helped his wife feed his daughter and played with his little sister Anya.

The room went silent, however, as Vasily entered with Dylan.

All eyes were on the curious pair, especially on the breathtakingly beautiful boy with his bright eyes and rosy cheeks.

"Good morning," Dmitry said, putting down his paper.

"Good morning, Boss," Vasily said, looking down at his son. "Everyone, this is Dylan. He's... my guest," he grunted.

"He's so handsome," Royal said in awe. "I'm sure that you're very proud of *your guest*." She had heard the entire story already from her husband and found it to be remarkable. Vasily had always been a very secretive man about his private life, never mentioning any family and especially any former lovers. To know that he actually had been in a relationship before made him more human in her eyes.

In appreciation Vasily nodded toward Royal. "Thank you for that. I'm growing quite fond of him myself. His mother is still asleep. But Dylan was hungry, so I thought... "

"Join us," Anatoly insisted, pulling out the chair opposite him and his wife. "Dylan come and sit with me while your... " There was an abrupt pause. He narrowed his eyes at Vasily. "*On znayet , chto vy yego otets* ?" Hoping that the boy did not speak Russian, he asked Vasily if Dylan knew that he was his father.

"Net," Vasily responded, a little embarrassed to say so in front of everyone.

Anatoly tilted his head, but decided against anything more on the subject. Certain things simply weren't his business. "Vasily will fix your plate," he said, taping the chair. "Dylan, you come and sit with your uncle Anatoly."

Dylan looked up at Vasily and waited for him to say that it was okay.

"Go on then boy," Vasily said, giving him a little nudge.

Dmitry's daughter was the first to greet him. Near him in age, she boasted the same blue eyes as her father and long black hair tied with a red ribbon that even when curled stopped at her lower back. She turned in her chair, ecstatic at someone new to play with and smiled at him.

"Hello," she said simply.

Dylan's face lit up. "Hello," he said taking the seat beside her.

"Are you going to live here now?" she asked innocently.

"I don't know," Dylan answered. "I'll ask my mom when she wakes up."

"What do you want for breakfast," Vasily asked Dylan, cutting off the conversation.

"Cereal," Dylan answered.

Dmitry laughed. "The universal breakfast of children." He winked at Dylan. "We've got a wide selection. What's your favorite?"

"Captain Crunch. I like the peanut butter kind," Dylan answered.

"I bet we have that, too," Dmitry said, picking his newspaper back up.

"Oh, I know we do. Anya loves it," Royal added, trying hard to hide her utter enjoyment of the scene.

"Alright, well, I'll be right back," Vasily said, glad that the hard part was over.

Gabriel watched the interactions between the boy and the family without a word, but when Vasily headed toward the kitchen, he excused himself from the table. Following behind him out of earshot of the family, he went to the counter to pour more coffee.

"It's always hardest for the last ones into the circle. I know. *Well, you know*. You were there when I had my introduction into the

Medlov clan. You might want to spend extra time with him so that he can get used to everything," Gabriel said casually. "It can be real a culture shock for a person to come into this world, but just remember that everyone comes around in their own time."

"Thanks for the advice," Vasily said, digging into the cabinet for a box of cereal. He didn't bother to look back or make eye contact.

Nothing new for Vasily.

"Anytime," Gabriel said, unsure if the normally stoic man ever showed any emotion. Walking out of the room, he left him to fixing the cereal for his son and hoped that he'd actually gotten through to him.

When Vasily was alone, he took a deep breath. It had been years since any attention at all had been on him, even in his private life. Now, his entire world and everyone in it was looking at him. Only, he wasn't concerned about himself as much as he was concerned about his son. It was hard not to tell the boy who he really was. Hearing Dylan vocalize at such a young age that all he had was his mother reminded him so much of his own life, something that he promised himself that he'd never do to a child of his own. Now, here he was.

How do I make it up to him? he asked himself, refusing to place blame on anyone but himself. Pouring the bowl of cereal, he tried to still his nerves. He had to keep it together, had to not be any different then he normally was. Only this family wasn't helping him. They all were so *family-oriented,* until it was hard to carry on the way he had done before.

The sound of the door opening again made him stiffen. He turned to see Royal with a clever grin on her face. She walked over to him and took the bowl out of his hands.

"Are you alright?" she asked him in a soothing voice.

He looked down at her and shook his head. "No. I'm still in shock, I think."

"That's natural." Royal walked over to the kitchen table and poured milk into the bowl. "You know, I didn't meet my mother until I was an adult *with a child*. Anatoly didn't meet Dmitry until he was an adult, and Gabriel didn't meet the rest of his family, to his detriment I might add, until he was an adult." She walked back over and handed him the bowl. "But you have a chance while he's still just a baby to develop a priceless relationship with him. Now all of this might be untimely and the way that you found out might be unfortunate, but it all happened for a reason. Make the best of it. Make it worth it."

Vasily smiled at her. "I will. I promise." Pride overtook him for just a second. "He looks just like me."

She chuckled. "Oh, Vasily. Don't be vain. He looks so much better than you." Rubbing his large arm, she motioned toward the door. "Let's go have breakfast as a family. Okay?"

"Okay," he said, following her out.

***

When Lilly woke up and saw that she was alone, it took her only a few seconds to throw on some clothes, brush her teeth and put her hair in a ponytail before she headed out of her room. As soon as she did so, she was met by a bodyguard in the hall who escorted her down to where the family was congregating.

The house was bigger than she remembered from the night before. In the daylight it was even more opulent and intimidating, but at the moment, all she cared to do was see her son and make sure that he was okay.

Hearing Dylan laugh at a joke by Anatoly made her heart skip a beat as she rounded the corner. He was okay if he was laughing. And if he was okay, then she was okay.

Again the room went silent when Lilly was brought in. They all looked at her with smiles that made her wonder if they truly were as nice as they seemed or if it was simply *rich people* manners. She tried hard to keep her mouth from flying open in shock as she looked around the table. Sitting right beside her son was Vasily and right by him was an empty chair in front of a table setting, she assumed was for her.

But the most shocking thing about the group were the other two black women at the table, one sitting beside Dmitry and one sitting by Anatoly, plus four interracial children outside of her own.

"Good morning, Lilly," Royal said with a smile.

"Yes, good morning," Renee chimed in giving an equally big smile.

"Please come and have a seat with us," Dmitry invited. "Did you sleep well?"

"I did. Thank you so much for your hospitality." Lilly made eye contact with Vasily, who as soon as he saw her felt his hands go clammy. He looked even better to her this morning, especially after the night that they had spent together.

Indicating that he wanted her to sit beside him Vasily pulled the chair away from the table for her.

A good sign.

She sat down and looked over at her son. "How are you, baby?"

"I'm good," Dylan answered with a grin. "Anya wants me to go outside and play with her later. Can I?"

"We'll see," Vasily answered for her. Passing her the container of orange juice, he gave her a warm smile. "Good morning," he said, giving her a look that let her know he wanted her again.

"Good morning," she blushed.

Lilly felt like a fish out of water, but she had to try to fit in. She wanted more than anything for them to like her, simply because they loved Vasily.

Royal spoke first. "I'm Royal, Dmitry's wife," she said, touching her chest with her mani-cured nails. As she did, the enormous diamond ring on her finger glimmered against the four-carat diamond necklace on her neck and the huge diamond studs in her ears. They were so brilliant until they flicked blue prisms against the crystal chandelier above. She wore a black tank top and black yoga pants, but even dressed down the coco-skinned woman with striking brown eyes, high cheek bones, smooth bone straight hair, perfectly arched brows and fire red lips looked like a supermodel, except for the large scar across the base of her neck. However, all of the expensive jewelry and her beauty made the one blemish on her perfect body seem miniscule.

"I'm Renee, Anatoly's wife," the woman sit-ting beside Anatoly said, waving at her from the opposite end of the table. Her smile was just as bright and pearly white. She was a darker and shorter woman than Royal, but just as beautiful. With glossy pouty lips, big almond shaped brown eyes and hair in a black asymmetrical bob, she had a baby doll face that was both warm and assuring. She wore a yellow cotton sundress and a gold cross but the wedding ring on her small finger gave away her low-key style.

They all were filthy rich.

The blonde on the end was the last to speak. "I'm Briggy, Gabriel's girlfriend," she said with a quiet almost wispy French accent. She was a beautiful woman with petite features and seemed to be the meekest of the group. Gabriel took her hand in his and kissed it, to which Lilly noticed that Renee rolled her eyes.

There was obviously a back story there that was none of her business.

"And I'm Gabriel, Anatoly's cousin, Dmitry's nephew, and as previously stated Briggy's other half," Gabriel joked.

Lilly thought that he was angelically beautiful with mossy green eyes and dark as night hair, but he didn't give off the same vibe as Dmitry and Anatoly. A beta male possibly. It was the command of his voice that gave him away.

"I'm Lilly," she finally said. "You've met my son, Dylan. We can't thank you enough for everything."

"Well, if you are a friend of Vasily's then you are a friend of ours," Royal said, smiling at Vasily as she said it. "And your son is such a well-mannered young man."

That made Lilly blush again. "Thank you." She looked over at him. "He's my world."

Royal liked that and everyone at the table understood it, except Gabriel, who was just glad the women of the family had turned their sights off of him for a moment.

"Now that we're all here, let's eat," Anatoly said, ending the awkward introductions. He knew that his friend was ready to move on past this and so was he.

Chapter 9

Brighton Beach, Brooklyn.
New York City

As the golden sun went down on the picture-perfect bay and white seagulls flew off into the distance over dark blue waters, trouble stirred along the beachside.

Off the boardwalk in one of the many small businesses that lined the community of Brighton Beach, Yakov prepared to close his butcher shop for the evening, a daily ritual that he took a great deal of pride in. For the first time in his life he was making an honest living doing an honest thing and closing his register no matter how miniscule the earnings for the day, was a direct testimony to that fact.

A lot had changed since Leo went to prison. Instead of taking over like many thought he would, Yakov hung up his gun belts and gave up the life that he had once known for calmer waters.

Now, he had bigger ambitions than being a boss, and they didn't involve having to answer to someone else for the rest of his life or have people killed.

Once he had taken Lilly to Vasily all those years ago, he returned to the only place that had been his home since he had left Russia, Brighton Beach, and met a simple girl from a simple family. At first sight, he had fallen in love with her and wanted to give her the world. Only, it would take time for his plan to unfold, especially with Leo only a half a state away. So, he kept his head down and kept his words few. He focused on making his wife fall in love with him and convincing her that he wasn't a monster. After a couple of years of courting, he married her. A year after that, they had their only baby. And when Muriel's father was ready to retire and offered to sell him his butcher shop, he bought it with cash.

The rest was history.

He didn't have to bother with hiding his many tattoos or his long history with the Vory v Zakone in this neighborhood, because Brighton was home. Everyone knew him, and everyone knew who he used to work for, but no one gave him any problems about it.

Yakov had developed a reputation of being one of the best butchers on the boardwalk, something that he took great pride in. And he even served cooked polish sausages and other meaty treats during his business hours for those who visited, an added service that the shop offered only after he took it over.

He was a family man now with a beautiful wife, a young son and a small but modern condo off the waterway.

With the television playing a TNT show in the background and the doors and windows opened to let in the peaceful late evening breeze, he helped the last customer with her order while his wife mopped down the checkered black and white linoleum floors with Pine Sol and wiped off the red countertops with bleach water.

"Spasiba, Mrs. Afonin," Yakov said with a warm smile. "Make sure to come back next week. I'll have some special cuts for you and your husband."

"Spasiba, Yakov," the older woman said, taking her meats wrapped in white paper in her shaking, wrinkled hands. "You're such a good boy."

"I try," he said with a wink.

"Well, I'll bring by some borscht for you and your family on Monday. I'll fix it just the way you like it, with plenty of cream," she said, putting the food in her small push cart.

"Do you need an escort back to the house? Muriel can lock up while I take you." Mrs. Afonin had been in the community since he arrived in the states and was something like a mother to him. Over the years, he had seen her grow from an attractive mother of five grown children to an aged, silver-haired grandmother of thirteen.

"No," she protested with a grin. "I've got my little friend with me." She tapped her purse. "Thank heavens for the second amendment."

He couldn't help but laugh. "Very good then."

After he walked her out, he turned off his red fluorescent *open* sign and called out for his son. "Stepan," he said, pulling off his blood-stained apron.

A little boy of barely five with wispy blonde hair and bright brown eyes stood a few feet down from the butcher shop bouncing a ball with his friends.

"Yes, Papa," the boy answered quickly.

Yakov leaned against the door frame, exhausted. "It's time to come in. Say goodbye to your friends."

"Yes, Papa," Stephan said, giving the ball back. In past his father's legs, he ran at top speed into the restaurant tracking dirt onto the shiny floors.

"Don't run on the floor. I just mopped it. You'll fall," Muriel warned.

"Sorry, mama," Stepan said, coming to an abrupt halt.

"Go to the bathroom and wash your hands. We leave here in twenty minutes," Yakov said, pulling out his keys to lock up.

As he stepped inside and closed the door, someone grabbed the handle, causing the bell at the top of the door to jingle.

"Sorry, we're closed," Yakov apologized. As he looked up, he stood stunned.

He stared right into the eyes of Leo. His old boss cracked a toothy smile of menacing proportions. With a New York Yankees baseball hat pulled down low to cover his face and pair of jeans and white t-shirt on, Leo looked like a different man from the guy who had been put away many years before.

Yakov's face turned a pale shade, but he kept his eyes blank. Pushing the door open, he stepped aside and let Leo and four of his men inside. Locking up behind him, he pulled the shades quickly.

Muriel was confused. The men didn't look like customers. In fact, based upon the size of them and their familiar tattoos, they didn't look like they meant her family any good.

"Who is this?" she asked, mop still in her small hands. She clenched the handle tight.

Yakov gave a fake smile, knowing how the truth would scare her. "This is Leo." He had told her the stories about his past life, along with all the gory details, as a way to purge himself of what he once was in order to transform into what he wanted to be. But never in a million years did he think that she'd be standing face-to-face with Leo.

The thought sent chills down his spine, though he did not show it.

Leo sensed Yakov's sudden concern. Tension was thick in the air, just the way that he liked it. "So nice to meet you," he said, offering his hand to Muriel. "And who might you be?"

Her big hazel eyes darted back between her husband and the man of her husband's nightmares. "I'm Muriel. I'm Yakov's wife." Her face gave away any misconception as to whether or not she knew who he was.

Leo gave a very dramatic sigh. "Well, give me a hug then. You're family for goodness sake." He wrapped his large arms around her and hugged her tight. Releasing her, he kissed her cheek. "Such a beautiful woman Yakov. You chose well."

"Thank you," Yakov said, back erect with fear.

"I would have sent something to the wedding, but I'm afraid I was bit locked up," he said sarcastically as he threw up his hands.

"Pity you got here so late. They are just leaving," Yakov said, looking at his wife.

"They?" Leo said, looking around the small store front. "Are there more?"

Nearly on cue, the bathroom door flew open and Stepan came barreling out, forgetting his parents' advisement for him not to run through the store. "Momma, can we stop for ice cream before we go home?"

Leo clapped his hands together. "Well, isn't this rich?" His baritone voice echoed throughout the building.

Muriel motioned for her son. "Come here," she said, grabbing his hand.

Yakov walked over and stood with them, over them. He knew his old boss well. If something was going to happen to his family, it wouldn't be with him across the room watching.

"This is my son," Yakov said, giving Muriel the keys. He clinched her hand tight for a millisecond.

"Hell of a boy," Leo said, narrowing his eyes on his old friend. "Hell of life, wouldn't you say?"

"You don't have anything to worry about here. They won't say a word. I saw on the news that you'd gotten out. Just figured that you'd be headed somewhere a little warmer and deeper south than Little Odessa," Yakov said, relaxing his shoulders. He sized up Leo's men. "Good to see you kept some of your boys.

They're not the best of the litter, but loyal all the same."

Yakov's change in demeanor calmed the men. He knew that he had to control the situation, had to make Leo feel as though he could trust him. If he behaved like he had done something wrong, then Leo might very well feel as though he had. And during his time with him, he'd seen more than a few men killed over a hunch.

"A man has to work with what he's given. So, then if you knew that I was out, then you have to know what I'm looking for," Leo said, sucking his teeth.

"Let's talk alone. Like I said, they are just leaving. I'll fix everyone something to eat. You have to be starving. And we can talk about what you came for, *da*." Yakov slapped Leo on the shoulder. "I see you used your time in prison well. You're huge."

Leo laughed. "Not much else to do in prison but work out and plot revenge." He looked back at Yakov's family and nodded. "Let them out," he told his men. "I'm sure that they are easy enough to find, should we need to."

Cutting his eyes at Yakov, he moved out of Muriel's way. "It was very nice to meet you."

Muriel nodded. "Thank you," she said, voice quivering.

"I'll walk them to the car," Yakov said, picking up his son and putting him on his hip.

He walked up to one of the men, who still stood between his family and the back door and stuck his chest out. "Instead of trying to be a bad ass, go in the kitchen and start the oven back up. I'll make us all some dinner. Plus, I think I have a few bottles of vodka hidden back there in the cabinet behind the seasonings. Fish them out, and we can catch up."

Leo laughed again and relaxed his own shoulders. "Do as he says, Taras, before he kicks your ass." Taking off his hat, he took a seat at one of the tables. "Go on Yakov. Send your family on. We'll be waiting." He tapped his hands against the countertop and threw his hands back behind his head to stretch. "Damn, it feels good to be back in the world again."

Yakov was quick about getting his family to the car parked out back. They moved quickly and quietly. And as Leo promised, he allowed him to do so without his men following.

Wiping the impatient tears that burned her cheeks, Muriel loaded into their black Yukon with her son and reached out for her husband.

"Should I call the police?" she asked.

"No," Yakov said, grabbing her hands. He kissed them gently. "Trust me. The safest thing that you can do is just go home and let me handle this. Wait for me. And if I don't come back, leave and go to your parent's house."

"What if he kills you?" she sniffled and looked toward the back door, slightly cracked.

"He won't," Yakov assured. He wiped her cheeks. "My beautiful Muriel. There is nothing to fear. I'm just going to go in here and talk to him. I know what he wants."

"*I know* what he wants," she hissed in a low tone. "Maybe we should just give it to him. It's not worth it to lose our family."

"No," Yakov said, looking over his shoulder. He put a finger over her lips to silence her. "He just wants to know where the girl is, but he can't get to her. She was hidden by Vasily, and Vasily is now with Dmitry Medlov, only Leo doesn't even know that he's alive. There is no way to trace her and or him. And if he does find either or both of them, he'll think that Lilly gave Dmitry and Vasily the diamonds in exchange for safety. And if I know Leo, he will go to war with Dmitry over the diamonds and the Medlov men will kill him. Either way, no one will think to look at us. And when Leo is out of the picture for good, then we can disappear and have the life that we've always talked about."

Muriel shook her head. "What if it doesn't work, Yakov? These are smart men and this is a lot of money. You said Leo would get killed in jail, and then we'd have the money. But they didn't kill him, even after you paid that gang. Then, you said his own people would kill him, but he showed up here tonight. Everything you have said would work, has not worked. And as much as I love you, you are playing with our lives. "

"It will work," he promised. Leaning in to kiss her forehead, he stepped back and closed the door. "Drive home and wait for me there. Don't call anyone."

The back door opened and one of Leo's men stepped outside. He looked over at Yakov and lit a cigarette.

Yakov knew that Leo had sent someone out to check on him and make sure that he hadn't run off.

"Go," Yakov said to his wife. "Now."

Chapter 10

Medlov Compound

The entire Medlov house was still sleeping, except two. As dawn approached, Lilly grabbed the side of the nightstand, grasping for air and let out another muffled scream.

Slow and steady, he continued, never looking up. He drank from her greedily, soaking up her essence as he fondled her. As he gripped her sides, he pushed his long, nimble tongue into her folds and flicked at her velvety plushness. Crying out in pleasure, she felt the familiar warmness begin to approach as he pulled her further toward the end of the bed.

On his knees by the bed, he focused on pleasing her. Sounds so raw and unnerving came from his efforts that it sent Lilly mad. His fingers stroked her as he lapped at her center, teasing her pearl and fingering her deep. Her body tensed with each evolution, responding to his unspeakable skill, just as he commanded.

Despite her best efforts to keep her climax at bay, she could feel the crescendo of violent waves as they beat against her inner walls. Her toes began to curl and legs began to lock. Arching her back, she felt his large palm push down on her mound and position her just where he wanted her.

It was a passion-filled torture that she happily endured.

Throwing her shapely legs over his shoulders, he moved deeper. With a sharpened tongue, he cut through her, watching her fragile wall begin to crumble. Then suddenly, the violent surge came upon her.

She shot up from the bed, back erect, legs straight, holding tight to his head as he picked her up and sucked at her madly. Unable to control herself, she screamed out and trembled. The orgasm was so spell binding that she felt as though she was floating, when in fact, it was Vasily who held her effortlessly nearly a foot off the bed.

As her body went limp, he placed her back down on the bed, legs splayed wide, inner thighs covered in her own silk. Convulsing, she reached out for him, recognizing for the first time his painfully erect manhood.

She rested back, panting and sweating, looking up at the ceiling and trying to put in words what her body felt, but there were none.

"Ponravilas' li vam eto?" he asked, voice deep and sexy.

She could barely speak. "Yes," she gasped for air. "I enjoyed that very much."

Before she could regain her composure, he stood up from his kneeling position and rested over her chest to kiss her while slipping his erection into her throbbing sex. Sucking in a fleeting breath, she held him tight.

He looked into her eyes as he took her, enjoying the faces that she made when she was in ecstasy. His movements were slow this time, certain that she had to be reaching exhaustion after their marathon sex session.

Still, neither one of them could get enough. For the last seven days, after Dylan was put to bed, they had snuck off to his room to enjoy what they had been denied for over eight years.

They held on to every moment, never missed an opportunity to be together. When he wasn't working, he was with her and Dylan. When they were away, they thought of each other. In just a short period of time, the connection had grown so strong between them until it was justifiable scary.

She held on to his back, nails digging into his skin as he hovered over her. With his hand on her hips, he pushed deeper and deeper into the plush velvet of her skin, feeling his own climax slowly approaching. His mouth parted as he ran a hand down her smooth stomach, planting a palm at the top of her mound to hold her into position.

Lilly could see it in his eyes, though he tried to fight it back. He was on the verge and so was she, yet again.

Planting an arm beside her, he lifted her thigh and planted his feet, quietly tensing to volcanic explosion. His movements became faster and harder. Pulling her closer to the end of the bed by her hips, his head flung back and he let out a growl that shook the walls.

His satisfaction made her smile. She loved to please him, couldn't get enough of feeling him inside of her or watching his amazing, rock-hard body.

Pulling slowly out of her, they separated but only to crawl into the bed. She pushed her back up into the curve of his chest and rested her head on his pillow. Breathing hard, he threw a large arm protectively over her and kissed the crown of her head.

"*Spasiba*" he said, out of breath. He closed his eyes and began to drift off for a second.

"You're welcome," she giggled. Looking at the alarm clock, she raised a brow. "You're not going to get any rest before you have to be up."

Pushing his hips up to her bottom, he sighed. "I'll sleep when I'm dead."

As the sun slowly crept upon the horizon Lilly felt her heart drop. She didn't want to leave him. "I guess that I should get up and get to my bed before Dylan wakes up."

Vasily's eyes flashed open. He didn't want her to go, but he understood. "Da," he answered flatly. "In a minute. Just stay here with me for a little while longer."

His request made her smile again, this time gratefully. Slowly, he was opening up, not about himself, but at least about how he felt towards her and Dylan. She only prayed that this entire, very temporary situation, was not giving her false hope. Neither one of them had broached the conversation about where this would lead. It seemed too premature considering no one knew where Leo was or what the final verdict of the situation would be. Or at least, she didn't. He'd promised her that when the time was right, he would repay Leo with the same courtesy that he'd given him 10 years ago.

Vasily's revenge is what she often referred to it as, that chance to make the things right that went wrong that night that he was shot. Lilly only hoped that his revenge wouldn't take him away from her again.

Feeling the ebb and flow of his deep breaths and warmth radiating from his body as he drifted off to sleep, she closed her eyes involuntarily and let their rhythms sync.

**

When Dylan woke up in the bed alone, he wasn't at all afraid. The sun was shining bright, and it was already seven o'clock in the morning, which meant breakfast would be served soon.

Grabbing the remote, he turned on the television and put it on Cartoon Network while he slid off the large pillow-top bed and made his way to the bathroom to change out of his Spiderman pajamas, get dressed, and brush his teeth.

All dressed and ready a few minutes later, he headed out of the bedroom, closing the door behind him, and excited about getting downstairs to see Anya. Today, they were playing pirates, and he was going to be Blackbeard.

As he passed Vasily's room, he had a thought. *Maybe he could see if Vasily had a patch that he could put over his eye*, since Royal had already given them a box full of fake jewelry to serve as their booty.

Going to the door, he twisted the knob but found it locked. Odd. Vasily never locked his door. He knocked on it lightly and pressed his ear to the door.

"Vasily," Dylan called out. His raspy voice echoed down the hall. "Are you in there?"

He knocked again, this time harder.

Lilly, still wrapped in Vasily's embrace, suddenly popped up, drenched in sweat and heart beating fast. Looking at the alarm clock, she shook him as hard as she could. "Vasily. *Vasily*, wake up. You're late."

Cracking his eyes open slightly; he looked up at Lilly naked and frantic and grabbed her by her hips. "Shh... it's okay. I'm getting up," he said in a groggy baritone. Immediately, his steely erection began to grow.

"No," Lilly protested. She shook him again. "Wake up. It's 7:00. You're late." She picked up the alarm clock and put it in front of his face.

Squinting his eyes, Vasily growled. "Shit," he said, sitting up.

When Dylan heard his Mom, he knocked harder. "Mom!" he called out. "Are you in there?"

Lilly bounced off the side of the bed and grabbed her clothes from off the floor. "Yes, honey. I'll be out in a minute," she called out in the sweetest tone that she could manage. Dressing as fast as she could, she whispered to Vasily, "How am I going to explain this?"

"Tell him the truth," Vasily said, slipping on his gym shorts.

"Which part? That you're his father or that we're seeing each other?" She let the words slip out of her mouth before she had time to craft them.

"Wait. We're seeing each other?" he asked, slipping a white cotton t-shirt. He closed the dresser drawer and looked back at her for a response.

The question stunned Lilly. Mouth flying wide open, she swallowed down a caught breath. Fearing she would stutter if she spoke, she said nothing at all.

Vasily couldn't help but smile. Casually, he walked over to her and kissed her on the crown of the head. "What's the matter? You don't know when I'm joking?"

She had to literally hide her exhalation. "No," she said, blinking hard. "I don't know when you're joking. You've never joked. Not since the day that I met you."

"I joke from time to time," he said with a shrug.

"Like once a decade?" she asked with a faux-frown on her face.

"I'm a funny man. People think I have a wonderful sense of humor," he defended.

"What people? Do you joke with them right before you shoot them so there are no witnesses?"

Even he had to laugh at that.

"I promise you that I'll tell a joke the next time that I kill someone. It might help lighten the mood."

He walked over to the door and waited for her to make sure that she was fully dressed before he opened it.

Seeing that she was as ready as she would be, he opened the door and looked down at his son, who was waiting patiently. "You're up early," Vasily said, motioning for him to come in.

"I've got plans with Anya," he said as he strode in. He looked around suspiciously. "Mom, did you spend the night in here?"

Lilly sat on the end of the bed. "Um... " she looked over at Vasily. "Mommy, stayed up all night talking to Vasily," she lied. "We talked in here so that we wouldn't wake you."

Dylan didn't seem the least bit bothered by the idea. He did, however, correct her. "Vasily said that I shouldn't call you *Mommy* anymore, just Mom. He said that big boys don't use that word. And I'm a big boy," Dylan explained, trying to seem as mature as his 70 lbs. would allow him to be.

Vasily smirked.

"Really?" she frowned. "Well, I'm sort of partial to Mommy."

He turned to his father. "What now? She likes Mommy."

Despite the small confrontation going on, Lilly couldn't help but stop and admire the two standing in front of her. Dylan looked so much like Vasily. Their stances gave them away. Both of them crossed their arms across their chests when they talked, and they both made the same facial expressions though they had not been around each other at all. Plus, more and more, she could see the connection happening between Vasily and Dylan all on its own. She didn't have to push it. It was just happening naturally.

After work, Vasily always found his way to where Dylan was so that he could talk to him. They had an hour-long conversations about nothing. It seemed that Vasily was trying to soak up as much as he could learn from his son, and she didn't blame him. It was horrible that she had to keep him away from Dylan for so many years, but she was also glad that he understood.

Her mind drifted off to what it would have been like to have been able to raise Dylan with Vasily, while the two stood in front of her discussing the wording of her title. And in truth, she was in bliss.

"Mom," Dylan said, turning to Lilly.

She snapped back into reality, concluding that *Mom* was here to stay and *Mommy* would be retired, at least until thunderstorms and nightmares came up.

"Yes, baby," she said, reaching out for him.

He walked over and slipped between her legs and wrapped his arms around her back. Resting his head in her bosom, he hugged her. "Are you coming down for breakfast? I'm hungry and like I said, Anya and I have plans. We're playing pirates today."

"Pirates? Sounds like fun," she said, standing up. Pulling down her wrinkled t-shirt, she tried to behave as though nothing had happened the night before with Vasily. "I'll just go and jump in the shower. And then the two of us can go to breakfast. How about that?"

"I can meet you down there," Dylan countered. "You and Vasily can come down together. I'm already ready. I brushed my teeth and everything."

"Is that okay?" Lilly asked Vasily.

"He'll be fine," Vasily said, headed toward the restroom. "Stop coddling him so much. He's a big boy. If he wants to go have breakfast, let him go. He's eight years old. At eight, I had a job."

"He's not you," she said, rubbing through his hair. "And we are in someone else's house."

"This hardly qualifies as just a house. It's more like a hotel," Vasily joked again. "He's fine," he said finally. "He's family. If there is some place that he's not supposed to go, he won't be able to get into that room. That's why they make locks for doors."

"Do you have an eye patch, Vasily?" Dylan asked, ignoring his mother. "I'm going to be Blackbeard." He followed his father into the restroom and stood at the counter.

"Come out of there and give him some privacy," Lilly scolded.

She came to the door to find Vasily had gone into a walk-in closet inside of the restroom instead of using the toilet, like she had thought.

Vasily stepped out of the closet. "The boy is fine," he said softly.

Dylan looked up confused at the two of them. *What was going on?*

"I just don't want him to get in the way," she explained, hands protectively on Dylan's slim shoulders.

Vasily looked at the two of them and felt sympathetic toward her. For years, this little man was all that she had. Of course, she would be protective over him and worried for his every move, but she had to let go of the reins just a little bit. And he knew that he had to help her.

He motioned for Dylan to come to him. The little boy did so without question. Rubbing through his curly locks, Vasily smiled at his handsome son, quietly very proud of him in so many ways. "Hey, I have an idea. Tonight, after I wrap up things with my boss, why don't we sit down, have a nice dinner together with all those Russian foods I told you about and we can have a discussion? Just the three of us, eh," Vasily said more to Lilly than Dylan. He looked up at her.

Lilly knew what he meant. He wanted to tell Dylan who he really was.

"Do you think that's wise?" she asked him, voice barely above a whisper.

Vasily smiled. "He's a big boy, right?"

"I am a big boy," Dylan protested.

Vasily opened his hand and gave Dylan the eye patch he had pulled from the drawer in his closet.   "Yes,   you   are."

Chapter 11

President's Island was a huge industrial park with nothing attractive to see for miles and miles around. Yet, the Medlov men stood out on the mud and dirt talking to the architect about how dynamic Dmitry's new building was going to be once it was complete. Rolling the blueprints out on the back of an F-150, they looked at what the 250-acres of land would like in a matter of 18 months.

"Now that we have all of our permits and tax abatements from the city, we can move forward," Dmitry said, leaning over the edge of the truck. "I want no expense spared. This has to be *the* state of the art arms facility in the country."

Anatoly was a few feet away by Vasily smoking a cigarette and pretending like he was paying attention to his father. However, he couldn't get his mind off the deal that they were discussing when Vasily found out about Leo escaping from prison. "We've got to make sure that the deal in Ukraine doesn't fall through," he said to Gabriel, who was busy sending texts on his phone. Instantly, he wondered if it was business related or the woman everyone knew that Gabriel was seeing.

"If we don't, we'll be broke," Gabriel said, not looking up from his phone.

"I don't know about broke, but a few million lights," Anatoly corrected. "I'm thinking we should send someone over there to broker the deal face-to-face."

Gabriel dipped his head. "I don't see why not. Sure." He felt Anatoly's eyes on him. He looked over at his cousin winking his eye. "Oh, hell no," he blurted out.

Dmitry stopped talking and looked over at the boys. "Is there a problem?"

Anatoly smiled sarcastically. "Not at all Papa."

Gabriel turned so that his back was turned to his uncle. "I'm not going to the fucking Ukraine. Get someone else to sort this shit out."

Anatoly raised a brow. "Well, who else would you recommend?"

"Vasily," Gabriel said, putting his phone in his back pocket.

"He can't go." Anatoly said in a matter of fact tone.

"Why not?" Gabriel asked.

"He's got his family to look after right now."

"And I don't?" Gabriel asked.

"You don't have any kids, and you barely sleep in the same bedroom with Briggy. I hardly qualify that as family," Anatoly said with a snicker.

Gabriel's lips thinned. "It's not like that. We're just going through something."

"It's been a year. It's either going to work or it's not. If it's not, then break up with her," Anatoly said, walking out of earshot of his father.

"Let's just set the record straight. My private life is my business. I don't need you to tell me what to do with my girlfriend," Gabriel huffed. "Before you married Renee, you literally fucked everything that moved. I seem to recall a New York Times bestselling author who got the title because you screwed her and posted it online."

Anatoly shook a finger. "It got her off my back. I screwed her literally, because she was trying to screw me figuratively. Let's not forget that she, like someone else here, was a cop."

"*Was* being the operative word. Some days, you make me want to go back," Gabriel snapped.

Vasily bit down on his lip to ensure that not even a breath came out. Everyone knew that this was an issue at the house.

For a while, Gabriel had been at odds in his relationship with the woman that he was seeing. She also happened to be a woman that Anatoly had seen before he married his wife, and while that had been no big secret in the home, it had not been the easiest thing to maneuver around.

"Just because you dated her... " Gabriel began.

"This has nothing to do with me and Briggy. It's about the integrity of the house. It's about everyone knowing what the fuck you do when you leave there and the questions that we are asked when she's moping around. Now, Papa feels like you should be allowed to deal with it in your own time, but that's because Royal doesn't talk to him about it. Renee, on the other hand, wears my fucking ear out every time she gets a chance."

Gabriel had heard enough about his broken relationship. He threw up his hand to silence him. "Briggy and I are working things out. That's all you need to know."

"That's all I *care* to know," Anatoly said, throwing his hands up. "But it makes a perfect argument for why you should go to the Ukraine and handle this deal."

"I'm not going to the Ukraine," Gabriel bit out. "And that's that."

"If you say so," Anatoly said, turning to Vasily. "Do you think we have anyone we can send that we can trust to handle this thing?"

"We have a couple of runners who are reliable. I'm sure that we could send them, but it won't be the same as sending someone from the family," Vasily answered. He turned to see Dmitry look dead at him. "I think he wants our full attention."

"Come over here and learn something," Dmitry ordered. "Stop arguing over there like school girls. Leave home *at home*." Evidently, he had heard more of the conversation then they intended.

"One second, Papa," Anatoly shouted. He pointed at Gabriel. "You're the lowest man on the totem pole, you make it happen. Either you go to the Ukraine, or you send someone who we can trust, but I'm not sending Vasily."

"Fine," Gabriel said, spitting on the ground.

As they all walked back over to the truck with the rest of the group, Vasily's phone went off.

Dmitry rubbed the bridge of his nose in frustration. *It was like having three grown sons instead of one.*

"Sorry, Boss," Vasily said, seeing the call was coming from a blocked line. He stepped over the patches of mud by the trees and took the call. "Hello."

There was a pause and then, "It's Yakov," the voice said.

Vasily looked up. "I'm guessing that this isn't a social call?"

"No. Sorry. I don't know how to say this but just to come out and say it. Leo showed up at my shop with his boys. Sort of made me remember the old times when you and I were running and gunning. He's got Taras with him now. You know how *special* he is. "

"He's a fucking idiot," Vasily said flatly.

"Well, the years haven't changed him at all. Look, Leo didn't come here for old time sake. He was running down Lilly. I told him that the story was the same. I went to find her... kill her and she was gone." Yakov took a deep breath.

"But?" Vasily waited, knowing that there had to be more.

Yakov's voice strained. "Why would Leo care? He's a fugitive with his face posted on everything in the country. Why is he looking for Lilly?"

It didn't make sense to Vasily either but much of what Leo had done over the years was questionable.

Yakov knew that he was taking a gamble, but he decided to make his move. "Well, the answer is that he thinks that Lilly has something of his... about $20 million in diamonds."

"What?" Vasily stepped further away from the small meeting behind him.

"When he got popped by the Feds, he gave her $20 million in heisted diamonds to hide for him," Yakov said, looking across the bedroom at his wife, who was packing their belongings as quickly as she could. "She evidently turned on him, gave him up to the Feds and had him locked away, and she took the diamonds with her."

Vasily's heart dropped. "Did you know that when you brought her to me?"

"Hell no," he lied. "I'd never heard of any diamonds before now. For all I know, he was just saying that as a reason to get me to help him find her, but there is always the possibility." Yakov made sure that he planted seeds of doubt with everyone to ensure a good rat race.

Vasily felt like he was being double crossed again, but he wasn't sure by whom. "So does he plan to come here?"

"He plans to follow the diamonds." Yakov slipped some clothes in a duffle bag. "Look, *brat*, I stuck my neck out as far as I could on this for you and for her. I have my own family now. I have to think of them." He only wished his friend knew how fluid that statement was. "I'm getting my kid and my wife out of Little Odessa for a while as soon as I make sure that he's already on the road. I just wanted to be the first to let you know. If you're smart, you'll put a bullet in his head and call it a day. Then she can start over new without worrying about looking over her shoulder every time that she walks out of her front door, and you don't have to worry about going to war with a complete sociopath. And if she does have the diamonds then, well, you guys can start a new life together after he's dead."

"I thought he thought I was dead," Vasily said gruffly.

"You work for Dmitry Medlov now. Everyone who is anyone knows that, especially your old boss. He found that out while he was still locked up. I told him that you must have survived the shot. I ditched your body and got back without checking your vitals."

"And Lilly?" Vasily asked, not worried about himself.

"This is the global age. Someone tracked her down for him through someone else's Facebook page or some shit. I don't' know. The point is that he has a last known address on her." Yakov wouldn't tell him that he had tracked her down a few years ago himself and gave Leo the information as a bargaining chip when he stopped by the restaurant.

Vasily had heard enough. "Let him come then. For 10 years, I've wanted to get my own revenge on him for the bullet he had Taras put in my back. But now, it's a lot more personal."

"How so?" Yakov asked.

Vasily didn't trust the man enough to tell him. After all, there had been many years between them. "Not important for you," he said, looking back at his boss. He had to get back to work and deal with this personal stuff on his own time. "Do what you have to do, Yakov. Get out of town. Stay low. I'll handle the rest."

"Sorry about Lilly. I guess she got over on both of us. Have you been in touch at all?"

There was a short pause.

"No," Vasily lied. "I put her on a train 10 years ago, and I haven't heard from her since."

"Smart man," Yakov said, feeling as though he had kept his friend out of trouble, even if he had thrown Lilly under the bus.

"Where did Leo say that he was headed?" Vasily asked.

"No specific place...just south."   Yakov would at least throw him that bone.

"I'll deal with him when he gets here."

"Take care of yourself, brat," Yakov said, motioning for his wife to head out.

"You too," Vasily answered.

As Vasily hung up the phone, he looked up in the sky and took a deep breath. She had hurt him once, pulled away from him, left him to bleed on the floor of her lover's house, and he couldn't help but wonder if she was playing him now. She could have had the diamonds hid until just the right time. Eventually, a man like Leo would get picked off by someone while he was in jail. With money like that, all anyone smart had to do was sit in the background and wait.

"Everything okay," Anatoly asked, walking toward him. "You look like you just saw a ghost."

Vasily nodded. "Yes, Boss. Here I come."

Chapter 12

When Leo pulled up to the roadhouse bar, packed with pickup trucks and American-made mini-vans, he took a second look around. Unsure if he was even in the right place, he stepped out of the black Yukon Denali that he and his men had driven half-way across the United States in and stretched out his body.

"This is rich," he smirked. "I went to prison and so did she. Good for her ass."

"The paystub at her house said that she worked here," Taras, one of Leo's men said, standing on the side of the truck to urinate.

As he unzipped his pants, a younger couple walked past them, cuddled up and laughing. The guy took one look at Leo and his men and made a joke to his girlfriend under his breath, then yelled out, "They've got a bathroom inside."

Leo's head snapped toward the man. "If you don't mind your business, then we'll use your girlfriend as our urinal, maybe you too, da."

The man quickly hurried with girlfriend to the car and got in.

Taras shook his head. "Boss, you might not want to make a scene down here. We sort of stick out, you know. Don't want them calling the police."

Leo knew that Taras was right, but having been in prison so long, it was hard for him to control his temper.

As they walked into the small bar, a country band was on the small stage in the corner playing a cover song by Led Zeppelin and in its normal fashion; it was packed to the brim with people.

With his four henchmen behind him, Leo made a b-line for the bar, where Logan was standing, rag in hand.

"Welcome to Cleveland's. Whatcha having there, chief?" Logan asked, trying not to make it look so obvious that he was gawking at the out of place group.

Everyone else in the bar, however, was not as civil. They gawked at the five brooding monsters and whispered among themselves. It was obvious to everyone that without saying a word, they were not from Jackson.

Leo looked at the selection behind the bar. "Vodka," he said simply.

Logan nodded as he wiped down the bar. "Any old kind will do or are you partial to one in particular?"

Leo leaned in toward Logan. "Well, now that you ask, there is one that I was looking for." With a smug smile, he pushed a picture of Lilly across the bar with a hundred dollar bill on top of it. "I'm looking for a very specific type."

Logan looked at the picture of Lilly in her wedding gown standing beside Leo and then looked back up at him. A flicker of distrust laced his southern good looks. "Shit, man. She's been gone for over a week from here. And we don't have no idea where she is." He turned from Leo and grabbed two bottles off the back bar display. Turning around, he slammed them on the bar in front of them. "Now, I got two types of vodka. This here is my top shelf; this here is the house stuff. Which one you in the mood for?"

Leo sucked his teeth. "Who would know?"

"Know what?" Logan asked, being difficult.

Leo over enunciated the words. "Who would know where I could find her?" he bit out, trying to control his growing temper.

Logan spotted the tattoos on Leo's arm and narrowed his gaze on the man. "You might wanna try the police, maybe. Dude, I don't know. She just worked here. It ain't like we were best friends. Now you gonna buy something or what? I'm running a business here, not a location service."

Leo contemplated his next action carefully. He could have very easily snatched the man across the bar for getting smart with him and bashed his head in to the white meat. But it was a very good chance with as many *good old boys* in the place as there were, he'd have to shoot his way out.

"I'm going to pass on the drink, Jethro," Leo said, snatching the hundred dollar bill up. He turned to his men and sighed. "Let's get out of here. This music is making my ears bleed."

As they headed back out into the parking lot, a small red headed waitress who had been listening and watching from the other end of the bar came running out of the front door out after them. "Hey, mister?" she said, waving her hand.

Leo stopped and turned to her. "Yes." *She would never know how her accent irritated him.*

"That $100 still up for grabs?" Approaching carefully, she pulled out her notepad.

"Depends," Leo said, tilting his head. "Do you know where Lilly is?"

"No, but I know who would. Her babysitter is an old woman who lives in the same apartment complex as my sister. She'd know exactly where she is and when she'll be back."

"Babysitter?" he frowned.

"Her son, Dylan," she said, like he should have known that already.

"How old is this child... Dylan?" Leo asked, stepping closer to her.

"Eight. He just had a birthday not too long ago. I remember because she took off that day to throw him a party." She took a step back from him, watching his chest swell.

"And the father?" Leo pushed. "Where is he?"

"Hey man, the only reason I came to tell you is because Logan after you left said that Lilly must have been your wife at some point. And Dylan is obviously not all black, so I just assumed… "

Throwing up a hand, he stopped her. "Wait. What does he look like, if he doesn't look black?"

She stuttered at his directness. "Well, he looks like you… well… "

Leo frowned.

She tried to explain. "Maybe not like you, but he looks white. Half white."

"Just give me the address… now," he said in a grave voice.

The woman did so quickly. At the same time that she tore the paper off the notepad, Leo pulled the money out of his pocket and dangled it before her like a carrot. Holding the hundred dollar bill in his hand, he slowly tore it down the middle.

Her eyes widened in disbelief.

"Half the information, half the payment," he said, throwing one half of it in her face.

She was about to put the paper back in her pocket when he grabbed her hand roughly and took it from her. "Thank you," he said, winking at her. "Let's go!" he told his men.

When he got in the backseat of the truck, he had to take a breath. At that moment, he wanted to kill Lilly more than he had ever wanted to kill her before. It was bad enough that she had testified against him and stole from him, but this was completely unforgivable.

"That bitch has my son?" he said aloud.

The other men were silent, giving their boss a moment to adjust.

Nostrils flaring, he passed the piece of paper up to the driver. He counted back the years to figure out exactly where he would have been when the boy was conceived.

Yakov said that he couldn't find Lilly when he sent him to kill her. Did she pay him in sex to stay alive? Was the kid Yakov's or was it really his. They had been together the night that he was carried away by the Feds. "Lock that address into the GPS and take me to her now. Someone is going to tell me what the fuck is going on."

***

Vasily had never looked forward too much in his life. In fact, it had been a comedy of errors for most of his adulthood, but earlier that morning when he gazed into his son's innocent face, he was looking forward to telling him who he truly was. Somehow the boy had given him hope, and whether he admitted it or not, all of the old feelings that he had for Lilly had resurfaced.

He had left with his bosses that morning in a good mood, though he never showed it, and was literally counting the hours until he arrived back at the compound.

Then he got the call from Yakov.

Now, his stomach was in knots and the questions that had lingered the first day that he had brought her and Dylan here were back on the table.

When they got to the house late in the evening after their many meetings in the city, Gabriel went to the home gym, Anatoly went straight to see his family and Dmitry hurried to the west wing to see Royal and his three children.

Vasily envied them as they went on about their night, knowing that regardless of the nature of their relationships with their children and the women that they loved, there was no question of their places in each other's lives.

Left alone, he grudged up the backstairs to his room trying to figure out how to handle the upcoming conversations that had to take place. Should he be direct? Should he be gentle? Should he even tell the boy who he was? One thing that truly bothered him was that if she would lie about the diamonds, maybe she'd lie about Dylan. Maybe everything was a lie, and he was just too stupid to see it.

When he turned the corner of the stairwell to head down the long corridor to his room, he saw Dylan playing in the hallway alone with a stack of Legos, waiting patiently for him.

"Hey," Dylan said, jumping up. He ran to him quickly and gave him a hug. Wrapping his small arms around his legs, he looked up at him and smiled. "Are you ready for our dinner?"

Vasily rubbed through his hair and tried to smile. "Yeah, about that… "

Dylan might have been a child, but he knew when someone was about to cancel on him. He cut Vasily off quickly. "Mom has been getting ready for hours. I haven't seen her since before Anya and I watched *Pirates of the Caribbean*, but she must be getting awfully pretty for you."

"Is she in there now?" Vasily asked.

"Think so," he said innocently.

"Hey, do me a favor. Why don't you go and hang out in my room until I speak with your mother? Can you do that for me? I'll come and get you when I'm done."

Dylan looked confused again. "Why, what's wrong?"

"Nothing is wrong, buddy. I just need to talk to your mother... alone." Vasily tried to lighten his voice. "I promise that I'll get ready right after. And I stick by my word. If I tell you that I'm going to do something, I do it."

Reluctantly, Dylan agreed. "Alright but don't be long," he said, twisting up his lip.

"Promise," Vasily said, winking at him. He walked him to his room, unlocked the door and let him in. "I'll just be a little minute," he said, urging the boy inside.

Knocking on Lilly's door, he waited for her to answer. When she didn't come directly, he knocked again. This time a little more impatiently. "Lilly," he said, suddenly suspicious.

Twisting the knob, he found it locked. "Lilly," he said, knocking harder on the door now. "Open up. It's Vasily."

Still no answer.

He took the key out of his pocket and unlocked it on his own. As he entered, he noticed the television was off and only a lamp was on in the far corner of the room by the window. There on the end table was a note.

If you've found this letter, then I've found a way to get off the property. I've been looking every day just in case, and it's a pretty secure place, locked down like Fort Knox. You won't understand this, but I have to go. I got an email from Ms. Clemmons, because it was the only way that she could find me. She told me that a man named Leo showed up tonight asking a lot of questions and threatened her. She told him everything that she knew to keep the other babies there safe. This won't end until he finds me. And now that he knows about Dylan, he won't stop until he finds him. Take care of my son for me. I'm going to finish this once and for all. I can't have him going after my baby, and I can't risk getting your wonderful family involved. I nearly cost you your life once. I won't do it again. I love you, and for all that you don't know I'm truly sorry. Love, Lilly."

Setting down the letter with shaking hands, Vasily picked up his cell and called down to Boris.

"Yes, Boss," Boris answered quickly.

"Did Lilly leave the property?" Vasily asked, his voice still calm.

"Haven't seen her," he answered. "Not that I'm aware of."

Vasily's heart dropped. "Pull the video from all the cameras and find out how she got off the property," he said, gritting his teeth. "Lock this place down now and send a team off site to the bus terminals and airport. Find her tonight and do it now."

"Yes, Boss," Boris said, hanging up.

Sitting down in the chair beside the table, Vasily took a deep breath. He had to get a hold of himself. There was too much to figure out and not enough time. *Why did she think that she could do this alone? What did she plan to do? What had she not told him? Why did she call Dylan her son?*

Tired of waiting, Dylan walked into the bedroom, holding his toys. "Vasily, where's Mom?" he asked. "Are we going to have dinner? I'm starving."

He looked at the boy, helpless and alone and knew that he had to be there for him like he'd never been before.

Straightening his suit, Vasily stood. "We're going to have dinner alone tonight, buddy. Just the two of us. Mom... " He paused. "Mom had to go and take care of something." He had just made a promise to the boy, and he planned to keep it.

"Are we still going to have that talk?" Dylan asked.

"We can have *a* talk, but *the* talk should wait for your mother," Vasily said. "How about we grab a bite and then I'll put you to bed. I have to go and take care of something."

"Like what?" Dylan asked.

"Grown up stuff," Vasily said, leading him out of the room.

Vasily knew that he had to find Lilly and keep her safe. He also knew that all those years of waiting to get even with Leo had finally come to head. Whatever Lilly had done or had not done, didn't matter. What did matter was that he had to protect what was his.

Part 2

Chapter 13

10 years earlier (2004)
Metropolitan Correctional Center
150 Park Row
New York, NY 10007

The overcast, dark gray skies, thick pollution-filled air and smell of impending rain added to the ominous task that Yakov had been assigned today. He had to go where no self-respecting Vor wanted to go, a place more contemptible than the four corners of any coffin but just as final for most. It was a place so dreaded that many tattoo had been created about it.

J.A.I.L.

Those four little letters when strung together sucked the life out of men like Yakov, and while many, including him, had done a stint or two there, no one ever wanted to go back, not even to visit.

Word had come to him through his boss sleazy, overweight, *overpaid* lawyer just this morning before dawn that his presences was requested. He was resting in his small apartment on the waterfront of Brighton Beach with three high-end escorts he had picked up the night before at the Rasputin Super Club when the phone startled him out of a peaceful slumber.

Still drunk, he had answered his cell phone quickly, knowing something had to be wrong.

"Da," he had croaked, scratching the blonde stubble growing back on his meaty, tattooed chest.

"Be at 150 Park Row by 3:00 today. Don't be late," the man had ordered gruffly before hanging up.

Yakov had hung up the phone and crawled over the women to get out of the bed and start his day even before the sun rose.

Now at 2:34 p.m. he pulled into a parking spot right in front of the building he was supposed to be at by three.

Blind luck to find the parking spot.

In every other way, he was not so lucky today.

Angry yellow cabs whizzed past him laying on their horns in the thick rush hour traffic; bikers jumped from the street to the sidewalk as pedestrians moved in flocks up and down the avenue, and he could feel the strain starting to form in the ventricles of his heart at the thought of entering into the fox's lair.

Getting out of his Yukon Denali, he pulled off his gun belt and threw it under the driver's seat. There was no way he could bring it inside of a law enforcement installation, but out here in the *real* world, there was no way he was going anywhere without it.

Pulling his black suit jacket off the passenger seat, he slipped it on, feeling bare without his gun holster under his arms. After a quick pat down of his pockets, he slammed the door, checked his hair in the window and hit the alarm.

As he entered through the revolving doors of the heavily secured building, he left behind the grueling summer heat. The lobby was cold, and sterile. Three guards in gray polyester pants, blue blazers with red embroidered writing and white cotton button downs stood at the security checkpoint waiting on him.

Yakov knew the drill all too well. He didn't need any directions.

Pulling his keys and wallet out of his pockets, he threw them in the clear acrylic box and passed it to one of the security guards to put on the conveyor belt before taking off his shoes.

"Before you ask, no I don't have any contraband, weapons, dangerous or illegal items," he snarled.

The female guard rolled her eyes at him as she lifted a brow. "Raise your hands for me. Legs apart," she said as she ran the wand over him before he could walk through the metal detector.

Yakov knew that wasn't policy — to be wanded before any metal was even detected. It was just another way to fuck with him. Still, he complied.

Stretching his arms, he was given the *once-over* by a middle-aged, heavy-set woman who obviously had smoked most of her life based upon the lines around her weathered mouth.

He could feel eyes on him from every direction — from the guards walking up and down the back of the lobby, the many cameras in every corner, the drug dogs a few feet away, and especially the three assholes right beside him. They were looking at his tattoos on his neck and hands, sizing him up, expecting trouble.

I'd love to give it to you, Yakov thought.

"What's your business here today?" a man sitting on a high stool at the end of the conveyor belt asked when Yakov walked over to collect his things. He looked at Yakov like he was trash and turned up his nose like he stunk.

"Going to see an inmate," Yakov answered as evenly as possible. He scanned the room again out of habit.

"Going to see a friend of yours?" the man sneered, giving him his wallet back. Before Yakov could answer, he pointed at the bank of elevators a few feet away. "Press six. Be prepared to show your identification as soon as you get off. They will clear you up there. If not, you'll be sent back down here and escorted out."

"*Spasiba*," Yakov said, cutting his eyes at the man. How he would love to meet him in a dark alleyway.

"You're welcome," the man said dismissively as he waved over the next man in line. "Over here, chief."

Twenty minutes and three pat downs later, a frustrated and sweaty Yakov was sitting in a booth waiting for his boss.

Leo was escorted into the room by two large guards. He was wearing a frightful orange jumpsuit and handcuffs around his wrists - a sight that made Yakov do a double take. Plopping down on the chair, he sucked his teeth and winked at Yakov.

They both picked up their phone at the same time.

"I'm surprised that they let you in," Leo said, looking around. His face wore his outward disgust that he had been reduced to such a shabby situation. "These motherfuckers are the worse. A bunch of bitches with badges." He made sure the guard could hear him. "They wouldn't be shit on the street."

"What about everyone else? Anyone giving you trouble?" Yakov asked concerned.

"No one is that stupid," Leo yawned. "They'd be dead before they could think it."

Yakov tilted his head in discomfort. There were more cops in this place than he'd ever been around in his entire life. "Maybe we should...speak in Russian, da."

That was worth a chuckle. "Won't matter. They speak that too. I swear, these bastards speak Aramaic," Leo said, pushing up closer to the table. His chair made an annoyingly loud noise as it dragged across the linoleum. He put his elbows down and turned up his lips. "I'm glad you're here. It really is a pleasant surprise and just in time. I've been worried about my wife." Leo smiled, as if she was the light of his life. "How is my baby?"

"Not holding up well," Yakov said, face tightening. "Or at least from what I've heard."

"Those fucking Feds are making her testify. They've scared her into it." His eye twitched. "Go to her. Tell her that I love her, and I un-derstand and tell her that everything will be okay. My lawyer is certain that I'll be out soon. Make sure she has everything that she needs, until I get home, and that ..." Leo paused dramatically and put his head down to keep from laughing. "Tell her that I love her very much."

"She loves you too, Boss. I'm sure of it," Yakov said in his most sincere voice, certain that the Feds were recording the entire conversation. "It will be okay. She'll be there waiting for you when you get out of here."

He looked back up at Yakov and narrowed his gaze. "We just got married, eh. She and I should be off honeymooning or making babies. Instead, these sons of whores have me locked in this place like a rat in a can, and they are waiting to put me on the stove, Yakov." Leo's chest expanded in pure rage. "They won't break me. No one will. No matter what. But in the meantime, I need you to watch over my angel." His gray eyes gleamed with malice.

Yakov nodded. "You know that I will, Boss." He ran a hand through his blonde curls, giving away his one nervous tick, but lucky that no one was there to notice it.

Leo put it on thick. "She's all I got in this fucking country."

"I know," Yakov said, taking a deep breath.

Shaking his head, Leo managed to push out a tear. "You're my *brat*. I love you. You know that, right? I mean, I can always count on you, and that means the world to me."

"Absolutely," Yakov whispered, phone pressed tightly to his ear.

Leo wiped his face and cleared his throat. "Yeah, well, I can't sit here and cry in front of you like a fucking *suka*. So, I'm gonna go. Thanks for coming to see me. It won't be forgotten." He hung up the phone and stood up. A wry smile of smug contentment crossed his lips as the guards approached to escort him back to his cell.

With his marching orders, Yakov stood up and straightened his suit. Leo had just made it abundantly clear. He wanted his wife Lilly dead ASAP, and he wanted Yakov to do it.

* * *

The Feds had offered Lilly everything but a new soul to get her to testify against Leo, but in return they had done a piss poor job of protecting her. Instead of taking her to a new location until the trial was over, she had opted to have security at her Manhattan home. Strangely enough, no one from the U.S. Attorney's office had any qualms about it. They gave her the standard speech about her safety being in danger and when she pushed, they threw up their hands, had her sign a waiver and posted three field guys at her house.

The three agents -were posted downstairs, while Lilly spent all of her time upstairs in her bedroom. Most days, it was impossible just to get out of the bed, but sometimes, she would make herself actually pack, a thing that was going to happen one way or another. Plus, it gave her something to do outside of regretting her existence.

At seven o'clock that evening as the muted sun began to hide behind the horizon of puffy clouds, the men downstairs settled in for the evening. It was the night before Lilly was going to testify before the grand jury, so a few additional men had been put in charge of watching the perimeter. But since all had gone well for the last six weeks, without one disturbance and Leo was still under lock and key, the level of intensity had all but gone away. At least, for everyone except Lilly.

Sitting up in her room in the dark, curled up in the bed looking out of the window, she waited. She knew her husband and knew that he would not let what she was doing to him go without retribution. However, running before the deed was done, would ensure his release. She had to do this- had to see it completely through, and if she lived through it, then she would run to the ends of the earth.

A strain was pulling in her chest from her racing heart down into her rigid spine. It was hard to breathe as she laid curled in the fetal position, still unable to move. Paralyzed by her own fear, she allowed hot tears to run down the side of her face onto the comforter. A quiet chaos was running wild in her mind, from one bad thought to another. The senses were a powerful thing. She could hear Leo's raised voice, feel the weight of his large hand against her face, see Vasily fly forward and hit the ground with blood spilling from his mouth.

A rap of knuckles on her bedroom door, made her move just a centimeter. An agent opened the door and looked in her.

"You alright there, Mrs. Rasputin?" he asked with a thick Boston accent.

"Yes," Lilly croaked out without taking her eyes off the window. "I'm fine."

"I've got dinner for you," he said, lifting up a plate. "It's the falafel you ordered from Mohammad's spot down the street."

"Set it down, please," Lilly said, swallowing down a sob. "I'll get it later." God in heaven knew that she couldn't eat anything right now. If she tried, she just might hurl it right back up.

The man frowned. "Hey, you alright?" He stepped into the dark room. "You seem awfully sad. Don't worry. You'll be safe. We won't let anything happen to you."

Carefully and cautiously, he walked over to the bed and leaned down in front of her. She looked up into his eyes and tried to smile. Her voice was nasally. "Thank you, Agent Sheldon. I appreciate your kind words, but I'm afraid that is just not true."

Agent Sheldon was an Irish, redheaded muscular man in his mid- 40s with a serious buzz cut and piercing green eyes. Boasting a gold wedding ring and smelling of family, he gave Lilly the feeling that he was a great dad to someone.

"You're doing the right thing, you know," he said, wiping a tear from her face. "Most wives just turn their heads and ignore what their husbands do in this kind of lifestyle, but you chose to testify, even when no one could make you. It takes an honest and special person to do that."

Lilly sniffed and raised her head just a little. "I'm not noble," she said in a matter-of-fact tone. "I'm only doing it, because I want Leo to rot in hell for what he did to someone I cared about, someone who will never have any justice or revenge."

Agent Sheldon nodded. "Well, you're doing it, regardless of the reason. That's all that matters." He set the plate beside her on the nightstand. "When you're feeling up to it, eat something, will you? You need all your strength for in the morning."

"I will. Promise," she answered, pulling the covers over her shoulders. "I just took a sleeping pill. I'm going to rest for a while, then I'll get up and eat. Thank you."

Rising up, he went over to the window and checked the boarded up opening. "Before you know it, you'll be back to real windows," he joked.

Lilly didn't respond. *Before you know it, I'll be dead*, she thought to herself silently.

That was his last attempt in cheering her up. It was obvious that Lilly needed to be left alone. "I'll check on you later," Agent Sheldon said right before he made his way out of the room, closing the door behind him.

***

Yakov knew Leo's home like the back of his hand. In fact, he was the only other person outside of his boss who knew about the passage way leading from the neighbor's basement into his own and then up a small hollow shoot of climbing stairs to Leo's bedroom. It was the perfect escape route; and the only reason that Leo had bought the house from his old boss before he got shot down in Brighton Beach five years earlier.

Tonight, he was using the entrance for one purpose – to get to Lilly.

Ignoring the rats, bugs and darkness, he made his way through the bricked, damp tunnels into the basement at a slow, cautious pace. Dressed in all black tactical gear with his two best Glock 19 Gemtechs with silencers, he moved through the darkness without detection.

Putting the small but powerful flashlight in his mouth, he pulled up the metal ladder stairs several flights to the opening that was Leo's bedroom.

From the inside of the room, the bookshelf appeared to be just an embedded piece of hard Maplewood furniture carved into the wall. However, from the tunnel, there was a latch that once unlocked opened the bookshelf without hardly any noise.

He made sure to listen first for any movement, conversation, signs of Lilly having company in the room.

There was no light coming from the bottom of the opening, which meant the light was off. There was no sound, not even of a television.

Unlatching the secret opening, he held the door as it opened, switching off his flashlight at the same time. Stepping inside, he closed it only halfway and stealthily moved over to Lilly.

She was lying in bed with her back to him.

He pulled his gun out of his holster and cocked it, as he did, Lilly rolled over and looked at him. Her brown eyes, even in the darkness, were locked on him.

Expecting a scream, he pointed the weapon at her and placed his finger on the trigger, but Lilly only sat up in the bed.

"Yakov is that you?" she said, moving her hair out of her face.

Her voice was clear as a bell now and innocent, a sound that sent a shiver down Yakov's spine. *Normally, killing women was not his thing.*

Yakov kept the gun pointed. "Where are the diamonds?" he asked. He had to remember to do everything in order. Leo wanted the diamonds first and then her shot last.

"Is that the only reason that you're here?" she asked, pulling the covers from her legs. She reached over and turned on the light.

As she did, Yakov's eyes trailed her perfect body, only covered by a thin layer of a satin robe.

"Why else would I sneak into a house full of fucking cops? Leo wants those diamonds," Yakov said, moving over to the door. He locked it and placed his fingers on his lips. "If you scream..."

"I know, you'll shoot me," she said softly.

Yakov walked over to the bed in front of her and tried to look her in her eyes, but it was nearly impossible to do with her chest rising and falling in nervousness. Her robe was open slightly, showing the roundness of her large aroused breasts. He could see the definition of her six pack and the firmness of her big baby doll legs.

Lilly might have been young, but she was no fool. She knew that look. And if she was ever going to have a chance at getting out of this room alive, she had to capitalize on it.

"Can I ask you a question, Yakov?" she said, spreading her legs apart so that he could see her perfectly shaved labia.

Yakov swallowed hard. "What?"

"Why are you so loyal to a man who would sacrifice you to the very men you are trying to save him from if he thought he could get out of jail as a result of it?" She looked up into his eyes. "You saw what he did to Vasily." Tears formed in the corner of her eyes. "You've seen what he's done to so many men."

"What makes you think I'm any different?" he asked, feeling a disobedient stir in his pants.

"Because you're here," she said, pulling at the tie on her robe. "Leo didn't deserve either one of us. Now, you're here risking your life for him one more time, when you..." She slowly opened the robe to reveal her naked body. As she did, she looked at the erection rising in his cargo pants. "You could just take the diamonds for yourself, let me testify tomorrow and put him away for good. Then we both could just start over brand new, lead our own lives. You get me out of here, and I'll never come back."

Yakov lowered the gun just an inch. "And is this supposed to sweeten the deal?" he asked, stepping closer to her.

Her brown eyes flashed with promise and determination. "I'm not going to lie to you; I want to live, Yakov. If you give me my life back, I'll give you the diamonds; I'll put him behind bars for a very long time and yes, I'll make love to you." She rested her elbows back in the bed. "I know that you want me, the question is do you want me more than you want to free that monster from his rightful cage."

Sweat had started to form on Yakov's forehead. Licking his lips, he took his hand off the trigger. "I want the diamonds *tonight*."

"Done."

"And if you don't testify, I'll come back here, and I'll kill you slowly."

Lilly clenched her jaw. "Understood." She watched him put away his gun in his holster. "Do we have a deal?"

Yakov crawled over her in the bed, covering her from sight. Dipping his head, he kissed her mouth slowly, moving her leg so that he could fit his large body between her supple thighs. "Yes," he said, sucking at her bottom lip. "We have a deal."

Chapter 14

Pulled away from their own families and their plans for the night, Dmitry, Anatoly, Gabriel and Vasily watched Dylan while he devoured his special meal of lamb kebobs, cucumber and radish salad and borscht with a dash of cream at the large kitchen table.

In the background, the television on the counter played highlights of sports segments, while they all huddled in a mass of testosterone around the boy, oblivious to his world bending around him, to protect his future.

While Dylan had never experienced Russian cuisine before, he seemed to enjoy it immensely. His face was covered with food as he dug in to the plates with the veracity of a grown man – much to Vasily's quiet delight. A belch half way through his meal indicated that his episode might be coming to an end. However, as he reached for the sparkling water in an ornate little crystal glass and took another sip then emptied more salad on his plate, it was apparent that he just might be getting his second wind.

They all sat quietly at the table, looking back and forth at each other and their cell phones, waiting for the boy to finish eating so that they could discuss the other business at hand, but Vasily insisted that regardless of what was happening outside of the house, he not go back on his promise to Dylan to have an uninterrupted and special meal.

Amazed at the boy's appetite, Anatoly finally broke his silence. "And when was the last time that he ate?" he asked sarcastically.

Dmitry smirked. "He's a growing boy. Growing boys eat."

"I don't recall eating like that at his age," Gabriel noted, utterly impressed by the boy's endless hunger.

"Mom said to always eat all of your food," Dylan said, looking up from his plate with a big bright smile. His green eyes sparkled like polished jade. "Plus, I'm never going to grow as big as Vasily if I don't get eight hours of sleep and eat plenty of food."

Dmitry raised a brow. "He has a point." With a smile, he played into the boy's happy moment. In truth, he liked children, liked their innocence.

"At the rate that you're eating, you'll be Vasily's size in two weeks," Anatoly said to Dylan, reaching over and grabbing a lamb kebob from the platter. "The rest of us might as well dive in before it's all gone. He's going to be here for a while."

"The food does look tasty," Gabriel said, grabbing a kebob also. "Plus, I love Gretchen's cooking."

All of the men grabbed a porcelain plate from the center of the table and started to top them with the food prepared by the chef. Relaxing a little, they bowed their elbows around their plates, all except Dmitry who couldn't fathom putting his elbows on the table during dinner, and settled in for a long night of strategizing.

"Where's the vodka?" Anatoly asked, scanning the table.

"There is some chilled in the refrigerator," Gabriel said, licking his fingers as he stood up. He came back with a large bottle of chilled Jewel of Russia vodka.

"I'll grab some glasses," Anatoly said, pushing his seat back.

Dmitry had a thought.   Putting his food down, he looked over at Dylan.   "Did your mother talk to Royal or Renee today?"

"Yes. They all talked for a long time in your bedroom," Dylan said, clueless as to why he was being asked questions, "but Anya and I had to leave, because they said it was private. And mom always says that children should stay out of grown folks business."

"My new favorite saying," Anatoly quipped.

Dmitry looked over at Vasily.   "There is no way to get off this property unless you are one of us.   Royal and Renee went to the shop earlier, did they not?"

Anatoly poured a tall glass of vodka. "Why would they help her? They barely know her."

"Never leave a house full of women alone unless you want a war when you come home," Dmitry said with a yawn.   "Dylan, are you getting tired yet?" He knew that he was.

The boy looked up with tired eyes, long lashes flapping like black wings, as he pushed away from the table also. He rubbed his tight little belly and nodded. "I think it's time for bed."

"You have enough?" Vasily asked without knowing he was being completely paternal at the moment.

"Yes, it was great," Dylan said with a proud grin. "I ate as much as you."

"More than," Anatoly joked. "But you did good."

"Boris," Vasily called out.

Boris, posted in the next room, turned the corner quickly and appeared in the room.

"Take Dylan up to his room and see after him getting ready for bed while we talk," Vasily said, rubbing through Dylan's locks. "Now, for the sleeping part to grow."

Dylan reached over and gave Vasily a hug. "Good night."

"Nite," Vasily said, hugging him back. "Don't forget to brush your teeth."

"I won't. Is mom coming back before I go to bed?" Dylan asked.

"Not tonight," Vasily said, refusing to lie to the boy.

Dylan cheeks blushed with embarrassment. "I know I'm supposed to be a big boy, but I don't know if I can sleep in that room alone."

"Take him to my room," Vasily told Boris.

Boris nodded and offered his hand. "Come with me, little soldier," he said, leaving the men to talk.

Gabriel chuckled. "Could it be, Vasily, that you've found your calling?"

Vasily made sure the boy was gone first, then ran a hand through his hair. "Boss, I need a paternity test." His voice carried his disappointment.

The room tensed at the words.

"I thought you knew for sure," Anatoly said deflating. He put down his food, feeling suddenly sick at the stomach.

"Things have changed," Vasily exhaled. He shook his head.

"Spill it," Dmitry said, pouring Vasily a glass of vodka.

***

A knock at Renee's bedroom door woke her from her peaceful slumber in her custom-made suite among dim mood lighting, plush carpets, million-dollar paintings, an impressive entertainment center, dozens of fresh roses and an attached nursery.

Sitting up beside the baby on the king sized bed, she wiped her tired eyes, trying to pull herself out of her fog. Glancing over at the digital clock on the nightstand, she yawned.

Anatoly would never knock on the door. It had to be someone else.

"Come in," she said afraid to wake the baby, rubbing her daughter's hair as she slept in a ball beside her.

At over a year old now, their baby had grown into a delightful bundle of creamy caramel joy with sandy locks, cherry red cheeks and pink pouty lips. With her knees pushed under her in her yellow cotton onesie and her hands under her chest, she slept peacefully beside her Mother in the dim glow of the beautiful room.

Boris cracked the door open and stepped inside slowly, knowing it was the baby's nap time. Out of respect, he barely looked Renee's way. "Boss Anatoly has asked that you come downstairs, please," he said as low as his deep voice would allow.

"What does he want?" Renee huffed, rubbing a hand through her wild natural curls. "I just got the baby to sleep," her voice strained in sheer irritation.

"I'm sorry," Boris apologized, raising his palms to her. "The entire..."

"Don't worry about it, Boris," Renee said, cutting him off. "I'll be down in a minute." She pointed her finger at him. "*But tell Ana* if this baby wakes up, he's going to be responsible for putting her back down, not me, and not Dmitry." Grandpa Dmitry loved putting the baby to sleep, and spoiling her and kissing her and allowing his son to get out of his fatherly responsibilities when he wanted to go outside and play with his dogs.

"I will tell him," Boris said, stepping out of the door without turning his back to her. As he closed the door, he sighed. "The Medlov men had turned this entire house into one big baby factory."

A few minutes later, still in her Snoopy pajamas and armed with a baby monitor, Renee arrived downstairs to the kitchen were Royal and Briggy stood, also summoned.

The three women looked at each other and rolled their eyes.

"What's this about?" Renee said, pulling a seat out beside Anatoly.

Dmitry was the first to speak. He knew who the ring leader was before he even asked. His wife was standing quietly in the corner making coffee with a smug, menacing grin on her face, like she had just spit in someone's soup.

"Now that we are all here, I want you to tell me where Lilly is?" Dmitry said, resting his large frame back in the chair.

Royal turned slowly with her mug clutched in her hand. She took a sip and quietly asked, "What do you mean?"

Gabriel cut his eyes at Briggy. "Are you part of this?"

"Part of what?" Briggy asked in her thick French accent. She kept her eyes on her coffee as well.

Anatoly shook his head. "Renee, what the hell?"

Dmitry knew the smell of bullshit, no matter where it came from. "No one can get off this property unless they are one of us, so at least one of us had to help her. Now, was it one of you or all of you?"

"All of us," Royal said, sucking her bottom lip.

Renee huffed. "Jeez, Royal, don't crack under pressure."

"Please, he already knows. That's why we are all here," Royal said, walking over to the table. She sat down beside her husband. "Lilly needed to go."

Vasily frowned. "Why?"

"Before you get to that," Dmitry said, raising a long finger. "What made you feel as though you were the one to make that decision?"

Royal rolled her neck and looked at her husband. "I'm sorry. Wasn't it you that said that we needed to help this woman?"

"Yes," Dmitry said, scratching his brow. His wife never ceased to amaze him. "The operative word is we."

"Well, did you ask *we* when you decided that she should come here?" Royal asked, softly but sternly.

"No," Dmitry answered.

"Well, *we* didn't feel the need to ask you to help her to leave." Royal looked over at Vasily. "She doesn't want to involve you anymore, Vasily. Lilly just wants to make sure that Dylan is safe. And as a mother I can appreciate that. So can Renee."

"Why would she not want to involve me?" Vasily asked, glad that someone could give him some insight into what was going on around him.

Renee chimed in. "After what happened to you, after all that you've sacrificed, she doesn't want to hurt you anymore."

All three women had been moved to tears by the story that Lilly had told them about how he had saved her and they also understood after she told them what she had done, why she felt the need to leave and do this on her own.

"How can she hurt me? Is the child not mine?" Vasily asked. He hated to know the answer, but he had to in order to move on.

Renee shrugged and looked at her husband. "She didn't say. She just said that she had to go and handle this by herself. And we could understand. That's why we helped her."

"All three of us understood. It wasn't that long ago that Briggy helped me get out of Prague to get to you in Sochi," Royal reminded Dmitry.

Dmitry felt a smile tugging at his lips. She was right as normal.

"This isn't child's play," Anatoly said, unable to be angry with Renee. Plus, this wasn't his fight, and *if* he was going to fight with Renee, he knew that it had better be worth it. She was hell on wheels now that she was his other half.

"Who in here is a child?" Royal asked.

Dmitry shook his head, telling his son not to go there. "Where is she headed, baby?"

Royal tightened her lips.

Briggy and Renee both looked away from their men.

Dmitry asked again. "Where is she?" he asked, putting a hand over her wedding hand. The heat from his body radiated on to her, melting her disposition slowly.

Royal rolled her eyes at the affect that he had on her. Damn him. "She wants to do this on her own. You don't understand."

"Make me understand," Dmitry said, with an even voice. "Don't forget that you are still my wife, and you may not owe anyone else in here an explanation, but you do owe me one."

Royal huffed. "She went to Chicago to confront some guy named Yakov about some diamonds she gave him to get out of town before her ex-husband was sent away. He evidently lied to Leo and told him that she had them. Well, she doesn't. She's flat broke. But at the same time, she can't allow that man near her son. Knowing that he's here is all that she needs. If he is safe, then she can focus on ending this once and for all. It was a mess that she created, and she feels as though it is a mess that she needs to fix instead of getting Vasily involved up to his ears again."

"How did you get her off the property?" Dmitry asked.

Royal knew that Dmitry wanted full and concise details. His ego would not allow anything less. "We sent her down the laundry chute that comes out right by the garage. I had Renee go and distract the security guy that watches the cameras while we snuck her in the trunk of our car, and we smuggled her out.

Even with the guys following us to the shop, they rarely watch the cars when they escort us inside. Once we went into the shop, she got out and hiked to the train station. We gave her some money and a cell phone."

Dmitry wiped his mouth and sighed. *This woman might be the death of him.* "I'll have Boris put a camera on the laundry shoots and the entire garage as well as have a man watch the cars at all times when they are inside of the shop from now on," he said, thinking more of how someone could have easily attacked them, if they wanted.

"I'll take care of it immediately," Vasily said, refusing to neglect his duties, even during this horrific moment.

"*Net*, you have other things to worry about," Anatoly growled. "Let someone else do the heavy lifting for once. Gabriel, you take care of it."

"Prick," Gabriel said, cutting his eyes at his cousin.

"What kind of phone did you give her?" Dmitry asked.

"One of the unopened drop phones from the stash," Royal said. "The *untraceable* ones."

"Does she plan to call once she arrives?" Anatoly asked.

"No," Renee answered. "The deal was to help her get out of the house. Now, she's on her own."

Vasily's face was blank as he tried to put the pieces of the puzzle together. "So, Yakov has the diamonds? He's had them the entire time?" Strangely, he was relieved to find out that Lilly had not lied to him about that, but he wanted to tear the flesh from Yakov's body for trying to set up Lilly.

Royal turned to Vasily with a look of complete sympathy. "It was the only way that she could walk away alive. She told us everything. And I in no way blame her."

"No one is blaming anyone," Dmitry said, pouring another glass of vodka. The last thing that he wanted to do was get all three of them worked up this late at night. "Where in Chicago is she going?"

"Where you picked her up," Renee said to Vasily. "Evidently, she thinks this Yakov character will go back to Chicago, because Leo didn't know about his place there. Lilly still remembers how to get to the condo. She thinks he might have the diamonds there and at least, she thinks that she can get them both in one place to confront Yakov about the diamonds in Leo's presence."

"Fuck. He's going to kill her," Vasily said, standing up.

Royal looked up at him. "You know, I know that we just seem like defenseless creatures, but we are not. If she left, I'm sure that she has a plan. She didn't tell it to us, but you have to trust her. She seems to be a very resourceful woman."

Renee looked away. No one was going to tell Vasily everything that Lilly had done to stay alive. His wrath might have been more than they could handle. Instead, they'd let him find out on his own.

Vasily had heard enough. "I need to go to Chicago."

"Take the jet," Anatoly said, standing up also. "I'll go with you." He felt compelled now more than ever to help, especially since Renee had a hand in things.

"No," Vasily said, shaking his head. "I'll take care of this myself. You've done enough."

"Just because you're not blood, doesn't mean you're not family," Gabriel said, standing and stretching. "If Charlie's Angels can stick their necks out, we can. I'm going with." He winked at Briggy, who blushed despite her issues with him.

"Well, I guess that means I'm left babysitting," Dmitry said, taking a sip of his vodka. "It seems we can't leave these three alone by themselves for five minutes. Go on to Chicago. Take care of this quietly and while you're gone, I'll get Dylan's mouth swabbed. By the time you get home, we'll know for sure."

Royal raised a brow to her husband but said nothing.

Vasily's heart broke. "If he's not mine..."

Anatoly slapped his old friend on the back before he could finish. "He's yours, regardless. The poor boy doesn't have anyone else."

Chapter 15

After a short hike down Main Street from Dmitry's Closet with a baseball cap covering her face and wearing a comfortable pair of jeans and white t-shirt with a light jacket wrapped around her waist, Lilly arrived at her destination.

Central Station was packed with people moving about preparing to board for the evening. It was a perfect place to hide out, a perfect environment to blend in. Most everyone was either cuddled up with a loved one or on their phones completely oblivious to the world, so it was easy to spot someone who was simply there on a look out.

She walked into the building and headed straight for the check-in to get the ticket that Royal had called in for her. *Thank heavens for friends or at least budding relationships.* Flushed with a roll of $100 bills compliments of the Medlov women and a secret plan that she had not shared with anyone, she pushed her identification across the table and gave her best fake smile to the older black woman behind the desk.

In all her years, Lilly had never been on a train. She had promised herself that she would take Dylan on a summer trip one day, but had never been able to afford it for the fear of being discovered. It was odd now that she found herself using such public transportation for such a clandestine mission.

Everything seemed surreal for the moment. This was the first time since she had given birth to her son that she'd been away from him for the purpose of a trip. For the last eight years, she had always been within 20 miles of him. And every moment since she had been away from him today, she had said a prayer for God to keep him safe.

Taking her ticket, she turned around and looked over the station. Even with all the people in the building, she had never felt more alone than at that moment.

She hoped her plan would work. It had to. She prayed that Vasily hadn't arrived home early or that anyone had told him where she was going. She prayed that Vasily would forgive her once he did figure out that she had left. More than anything, she prayed that she would be able to return to her son and the hope of something more with the man she had fallen so deeply in love with.

Grabbing a seat on one of the old wooden benches, she pulled out a sandwich she had packed in her backpack and nibbled on it, hoping it would sate the rampant butterflies erupting violently in her empty stomach.

A few hours later, she loaded on with the rest of the passengers headed to Chicago with only her small backpack thrown over her shoulder.

Glad to be moving, she presented her ticket again to the attendant along with her identification and was pointed in the direction of her superliner roomette, per Royal's suggestion. "You don't want to be out in the elements considering your situation," she had said. "Trust me, this is best."

Lilly stepped inside the small compartment and threw down her bag, then took a seat in one of the spacious reclining seats by the window. Grateful to be out of the large crowd, she pulled off her baseball cap and scratched threw her sweaty head.

Reaching into her pocket, she pulled out the cell phone that Royal had given her and a number she had pulled off the Internet. She tried to dial the number, but her nervousness overtook her. Unfortunately, she had not stopped trembling since she had gotten the email about Leo earlier. Every time, she thought about that man getting a hold of her son, she nearly went into a panic attack mode. Still, she had to press on until this was done.

Taking a deep breath and closing her eyes, she listened to her heartbeat in her ears go from a thud to a simple beat. Then she tried again. Dialing the number slowly, she pressed it up against her ear and waited.

The phone rang for just a moment before a dispatcher picked up.

"Federal Bureau of Investigation – Manhattan office. How may I help you, sir or ma'am?"

Lilly almost hung up the phone, but a picture of Dylan's face flashed through her mind.

"May I please speak to Agent Sheldon," Lilly stuttered.

There was a pause on the phone. "Hold please for Special Agent in Charge," the voice corrected before she was placed on a brief hold.

The voice came back. "Whom may I ask is calling?"

Lilly had not used her real name in so long until it sounded impossible to use. "Lilly Rasputin," she said, voice trembling.

"Hold please," the voice said, sounding a little more eager to help her.

Only a few seconds later, a familiar voice answered the phone.

"Lilly, is it really you?" Agent Sheldon asked.

"In the flesh," Lilly laughed nervously.

"Where are you? How are you?" Agent Sheldon asked, pulling his seat out. He sat down and grabbed a pen.

"I'm in Memphis, headed to Chicago." Heaving a sigh, she clasped her hands together. "How's life been treating you?"

"Well," he said, surprised that she would even ask. "Kids are gone to college and the wife and I are happy empty nesters."

"I'm happy for you," Lilly said sincerely. She looked out of the window as the train began to move. "I'm scared, Sheldon."

"Why? Has Leo contacted you?"

"He came looking for me." Lilly swallowed down her fear. "Before he was arrested, I hid $20 million in heisted diamonds for him. I used them as bargaining chips the night his right hand, Yakov, came to kill me. It was the same night that you came up and talked to me in my room. Do you remember that?"

"Of course, I do. You were shaking like a leaf. Wait," he paused. "Yakov was there?"

"Yes, I didn't realize it until after you had gone."

A chill went down Sheldon's spine.

"Leo wants the diamonds. He found me in Mississippi, but I was already gone."

Sheldon was nearly lost for words. He had been looking for her for nearly a decade, and suddenly she just popped up. He had so many questions, but he settled for just asking the most important ones for the moment. "Where did you run to? Who do you know in Memphis?"

"No one," Lilly lied. "I just went to the biggest city I could find. Memphis was the closest."

Sheldon knew that she wasn't telling the truth. "Why are you going to Chicago?"

"I think Yakov is going there. He has a place that maybe he's going to. I need to get there and find out if he has the diamonds. I also need to flush Leo out. So, I need him to know where I'm going."

"So, let me get this straight. You gave Yakov the diamonds?"

"Yes, but Leo thinks that I have them. Yakov must have lied and kept them for himself."

"Leo must be flat broke then," Sheldon said, strategizing as he talked. "Do you know who he heisted the diamonds from?"

"Florshiem's Jewelers in Manhattan. He and Yakov set up the heist and carried it out with their men the week before he was arrested."

Sheldon knew the case. The owner, his wife and two other men had been gunned down during the robbery; over $50 million worth of jewelry had been stolen from the safe.

"Those diamonds are traceable, Lilly. If we can put Yakov with the diamonds, then we can arrest him."

"I know," Lilly said, hoping he finally got why she was calling him. "Two birds...$20 million in stones."

"Can I reach you at this number in 10 minutes? Are you safe?" Sheldon asked, knowing that this bust was a career booster.

"I'm on a train headed from Memphis to Chicago. I'm not going anywhere for the next 10 hours," she said, feeling a small relief to know that he'd be willing to help her.

"I'll call you right back. I promise," Sheldon said, hanging up the phone.

Chapter 16

If there was one thing that Anatoly knew, it was his wife. Renee would have never stuck her neck out for a woman that she didn't know unless there was some serious, life-altering reason behind it. And he intended to find out why but in a more intimate setting than his kitchen.

However, like everything to do with Renee, it would take finesse. A man just couldn't walk in demanding things from her. Otherwise, he'd pull back a nub.

He had learned this the hard way on several occasions during his honeymoon phase where a slip of the tongue had been as fatal for him as feeding a hungry lion raw bloody meat with his bare hand. And even that was probably not as dangerous as provoking his young beautiful bride.

She was being groomed by his hellcat of a stepmother, Royal. And while Royal was only two-years older than him chronologically, she had an old woman's mind about how to keep her home in order. Plus, Renee was three years older than him, a dynamic that only came to play when she wanted to be *right*.

The familial structure of the house was somewhat complicated. Everyone had a wing, a domain, a safe area where they were able to be at peace and spend time with their families alone. However, overall his father ran everything, followed by himself, then Gabriel and then Vasily.

Unofficially, it felt as though the women ran everything. The old saying happy wife, happy life had never been familiar to him until he married. Now, it was his day-to-day mantra.

Anatoly had asked his father once, did he think it was a problem – the women and their politics. But Dmitry found it comical and explained that while their wives could have the entire world, they had to try to enjoy it on a little island, completely isolated from everyone else because of the lifestyle of the Medlov men, and the dangers that surrounded them.

"If they want to run their house, let them. We're barely here anyway and when we are, they spend all of their time catering to us and our children," Dmitry had explained almost in the form of a guilt trip. "Besides, you'll get used to it and believe it or not, start to depend upon it. There are other things that need your attention to detail. Leave the peas to the women and focus on the steak."

As usual, his father made perfect sense, something else that he had become accustomed to, so Anatoly had digressed.

After the small meeting in the kitchen, the women had excused themselves back upstairs to their children, Renee rushing faster than anyone to get to their daughter, and the men had been left to talk.

There was, however, little to say. He along with Gabriel and Vasily would be going to Chicago within the hour and his father would stay to protect the house and their children.

Dragging his exhausted body up the stairs to his wing of the house, he felt the pull of his bed even from down the hall. He wanted to rest, but he'd have to do it on the private jet. He was sure that Renee would pack him a bag and Boris was busy packing munitions and getting in touch with the Chicago family and preparing for their arrival.

Now, he only had a short time, less than 60 minutes to see precious little princess one last time before he slipped out for the night in hopes that they'd wrap this up quickly and return within the next day or two.

He slipped into their dimly lit bedroom and found Renee in the adjoining nursery lingering over the white hand-carved, wooden cradle that he had ordered from Moscow. She was humming a lullaby to their daughter, Alexandria, who slept peacefully under a soft cotton pink sheet.

This was the part of his life that was so different from everything else. In this room filled with all things Alexandria, like the changing table, diaper disposal, high chair, rocking chairs, the umpteen toys, the pictures in frames on the walls, the pink curtains matching the pink and green walls, the bears, the books and the little bitty clothes – this was a different world from anything that he knew, and he held it dear. Here, he wasn't a boss; he wasn't a criminal, and he wasn't second-in-charge of a multinational crime syndicate. Here he was daddy and husband. Nothing more, nothing less.

And in feeling that, how could he not understand why Vasily had to go after Lilly, why his father had gone after Royal, why he had gone after Renee, why they all had gone after Anya, and why it was of utmost importance to protect all five of the children who depended on them for safety from a world of men who would do them harm just for the pleasure of knowing what it would do to their fathers?

All they had in this world was each other. This island.

Wrapping his arms around Renee's waist, Anatoly nuzzled his head into her hair and rubbed his hands against the small pooch of her stomach.

"Are you mad at me?" she whispered.

"No," he said, kissing her neck. "It takes a little more than that to make me angry at you, but I think that you know that. That is why you did it."

A smile crept across her lips at the sound of his deep, sexy baritone and the fact that he was telling the truth.

"You know, I never would have helped her if it meant putting you in harm's way," she said, turning toward him. Her face was sincere, regretful even. "I just assumed you'd let her go, or let Vasily go after her."

Anatoly slipped his hand behind her small neck and pulled her face close. Her perfume tickled his nose and he inhaled greedily unable to get enough of her. "Are you doubting my mad skills all of a sudden," he asked playfully, words laced with passion.

She looked up into his cobalt blue eyes and felt butterflies erupt in her stomach. Amazingly, even after being married for a year, she still had a crush on him. Maybe it was his bad boy swag or his dirty blonde hair or his infinite muscles or his tattoos, but the look of him still drove her mad.

"No, I'm not doubting your mad skills," she whispered back. "I just don't like to provoke you into using them." The admiration in her eyes was unmistakable and the only thing that made Anatoly feel like a champion. It also made him want to dominate her physically.

Stepping into her, he dipped his head and kissed her full lips deep and long. His sweet, minty tongue cut like a hot knife on butter through her clever words and locked around her own as their mouths melted together.

In the darkness of the nursery while the mobile above the crib played a lullaby, Anatoly held her close and violated her senses with the promise of a sweet surrender on the horizon.

He kissed her so deeply until she literally forgot herself. She went limp in his warm and safe embrace. His large, roaming hands crushed into her and pulled her up against his growing erection.

Finally, when he released her after she was wet and disoriented; she realized that he was using yet another one of his skills against her.

"What do you want, Ana?" she asked, blinking hard.

Anatoly spoke softly, with her taste still upon his lips. "What don't I know," he asked, "about Vasily? What don't I know?" His plead was intense on Renee's heart. When they married, they made a covenant that required her loyalty to be first to him. Yet this was hard to repeat.

Renee heaved a breath and stepped around his large heaving frame. HWalking back into their bedroom to make sure that they didn't wake the baby, she stood in front of the bed with her fingers knitted.

Anatoly followed after her. Closing the door quietly behind him, he waited. The hesitation in her eyes told him that she was going to tell him something that he truly did not want to hear, still Vasily was his brat. He had to know what they were walking into and why.

Renee put her hands on her shapely hips – a sign that she was defensive. "Lilly loves him, you know. She truly loves him. It's the only reason why she went to do this alone. She couldn't bear the idea that anything might happen to him."

Anatoly didn't have anything to argue with about that. "Well, Dylan is her son. I would imagine..."

"No," Renee said, shaking her head. "She loves Vasily. She's always loved him. That's why she testified in court against the family. She thought Leo had killed him."

"He nearly did," Anatoly said, letting her know that he was aware of at least that part of the story. "But what doesn't she want him to know. Is Dylan his?" Anatoly's eye twitched.

Renee twisted up her lips. "She would have never made it to the witness stand if she hadn't given Yakov the diamonds."

Anatoly narrowed his eyes on his wife. "Still not enough of a reason to go at it alone."

Renee finally let it go. "She had to sweeten the deal."

The silence in the room was deafening.

Anatoly chest began to swell in anger. His fists balled and a vein began to protrude out the side of his neck. "If you're telling me that Dylan is Yakov's son, I'm going to fucking throw up. Vasily's been through enough hell..."

"No," Renee said, halting his ramping fury in mid-escalation. "Well, I don't know." She shrugged, frustrated. "She didn't say. I mean, she may know, I just don't."

"You're rambling," Anatoly reminded. His head snapped. "So he fucked her?"

Renee frowned. "I hate when you use a sewer mouth, Ana."

"Well, it's not like he made love to her, did he?" he asked sarcastically.

He had had a point. Renee rolled her eyes. "She just said it took a little more than diamonds to persuade him. She didn't lay out the details."

Anatoly scratched his head. That could have meant a laundry list of sexual favors all that would send his best friend off the deep end. "Vasily is going to fucking flip."

"That's why she didn't tell him. She just left. She knew Dylan would be safe here with us." Renee walked over and put her hand on Anatoly's rock hard chest. Her physical contact with him began to calm him down. "Ana, you can't let him find out yet. He might not help her."

"Is that what you're worried about?" Anatoly asked. *Renee evidently didn't know Vasily very well. He would follow Lilly to ends of the earth.*

"Yes," Renee answered. For good measure, she tried to relate. "You know, I would have done the same thing if I were her, in her exact situation. To protect your life you'll do just about anything."

Anatoly's gaze was intense again. "Shit... and you wonder why I keep you under lock and key."

Renee couldn't tell if he was joking or not, but she knew not to push her husband on the matter. Anatoly had always been territorial. He didn't like anyone even looking at her, so the conversation about her being with another man was inconceivable to him. Still, she had to make him see why Lilly wasn't to blame.

"So what's her plan?" he asked, looking at his watch. His 60 minutes had turned into 45.

"I told you, she didn't say. All we know is that she took a train to Chicago, headed to Yakov's old place."

"Hopefully not to fuck him again," Anatoly said, knowing that would piss Renee off. *Serves her right though for helping Lilly behind his back.*

Renee's mouth popped open. "Don't be like that." Turning to walk away, she felt him.

"Where are you going?" Anatoly grabbed her arm.

"To pack your bags," she said, looking at his hand on her.

Anatoly pulled her back toward him roughly. "Lilly is not the only one who has to sweeten the deal to get what she wants around here."

A faux look of disbelief crossed her face. "Are you really bribing me? Your wife?"

"Do you want me to help her or not?" Anatoly asked, face serious. "She's your girl, not mine. I don't know her. *I don't care to know her.* You black women are all trouble anyway."

"Funny. It seems like your house is nearly full with black women." She cracked a smile. "You would leave her there alone if I don't have sex with you?" She stepped closer to him, feeling his body heat as she closed her proximity. "Are you that much of an ass?"

"I will fucking shoot her myself if you don't have sex with me," he said, his expression inscrutable.

"Can't say that I'm surprised," Renee quipped. "You are a monster."

He picked her up off the floor and held her in his arms. "I'm going to teach you a lesson about what happens when you stick your nose into other people's business."

"Oh really," she taunted in anticipation, as he laid her across the bed.

Provocatively, he pulled off his t-shirt to reveal tanned, lean muscle. She ran her hand over her name tattooed on his chest. "You know I'm hard to teach," she said, as he crawled over her naked.

"Well, I'm just *hard*," he whispered in a rasping voice, putting her hand on his steely manhood. "We'll just have to see, if there is a common ground we can reach."

Renee giggled when she felt him pull her pants down with one hand. "Ana!" she laughed

Chapter 17

Gabriel looked down at his Presidential Rolex one more time as he listened to Briggy curse him in French across the bedroom. Throwing his clothes in a duffle bag, one article at a time, she growled in her deepest voice.

Her long, manicured nail pointed directly at him. "And I know that you've been sleeping with someone else. The entire house knows it. You make a complete mockery of me!" she said, tears rolling down her face. She grabbed a pair of black Calvin Klein briefs and waved them in the air. "I can smell sex on you when you come home...your expensive whore and her expensive perfume!" In her rage, her blonde tendrils bounced wildly across her like Medusa's locks of snakes, only her gaze had far more rage tonight then Gabriel could imagine any demi-goddess could have.

Briggy had never been *this* angry before. At least, not that he'd seen. Normally, she was a demure, quiet woman who voiced her objections reasonably. *Normally.*

However, they came into the room after the meeting in the kitchen, and he asked her why she felt the need to help Lilly. It was then that Briggy exploded. She turned deep red, burst into tears and started to scream at him.

Now, trying to calm her down was like trying to fit lighting into a bottle.

Gabriel didn't want this for her. And in truth, he didn't want this for himself. Still, he felt incredibly responsible for her. She didn't have any family. She was thousands of miles away from her home country. And most importantly, she was a known Medlov consorter. Basically, she was a moving target, and it was his job to keep her safe, even if she was not the woman that he wanted anymore.

Walking over to the disheveled bed, he placed his large hands on her shoulders and stopped her mid-rage. "Briggy, *baby*, we have to stop this." His voice was calming, soothing almost, despite this all being his fault.

"Don't *baby* me," she sobbed. "Why do you take so much pleasure in hurting me? What have I done, but love you, Gabriel?"

"You don't love me," he croaked. Damn, it felt good to say it for once. Anatoly was right and his words had lingered on his mind since their conversation, making life almost unbearable. He had to tell Briggy the truth. She deserved at least that from him.

"How can you say that?" Her blue eyes were blood shot. Caught off guard, her face twisted into a mix of confusion and pain. For a minute, she stopped breathing all together.

"I can say it because I don't love you, Briggy. I don't. I want to. I do," he said touching his chest. "It kills me that I can't. I'm...I'm fucking ashamed of it. You are a good woman. You deserve better, but I just...I don't love you."

Her eyes widened. "Then why did you ever take me?"

Gabriel mossy green eyes were wide with adrenaline. "I had my own selfish reasons, none of which are good enough to defend what I've done to you."

"Done to me?" she repeated. "Done to me? Êtes-vous sérieux? You have ruined me! You and your miserable cousin have ruined my life!" Her tears multiplied. "You have used me; you have disregarded me..."

"Briggy stop," Gabriel begged, guilt-ridden.

"And you think it's okay, because I'm not them. I'm not Royal, and I'm not Renee. I'm just your live-in girlfriend.   Some additional amenity to your lavish lifestyle...in house pussy! Dmitry warned me. He begged me not to consort with you boys, but I didn't listen. *Je pensais que tu m'aimais.*"

Wiping more tears, she looked at the diamond bracelet on her wrist and pulled it off. Throwing the bracelet at him, she cursed again. "You give me all of this...all of these things that I could never afford on my own, just to make me realize what would happen if you left me. Then you treat me like shit to show me how much you don't want me. You're as psychotic as your fucking father. Maybe worse!"

Gabriel tried, though it was difficult, to ignore her harsh comments of him.

"I give you these things because I want to." He bent and picked up the $100,000 bracelet and set it carefully on the bed.

In his voice, she could hear that she had hit a nerve and in her despair, it seemed to ease her hysteria to hurt him.

"You give them to me because Dmitry and Anatoly give them to their wives," Briggy hissed.

"I appreciate your candor but…"

"Don't do that!" Briggy pushed him as hard as she could, but he did not even flinch. At nearly seven feet tall and 290 pounds of pure muscle, it really was as if she was pushing against a brick wall. "You always say something smug when you want to berate me!"

"I'm not…"

"Why did you not come home again last night?" she asked, getting down to the root of the problem.

Gabriel looked away. *Did she really want him to say why?*

"Look at me, you fucking bastard!" She hit him again, this time with a closed fist.

Gabriel sighed and stepped back. Wiping his nose, he picked up the poorly packed bag. "I don't have time for this. When I get back, *then* we can talk."

"I don't want to talk anymore," she screamed. "I'm tired of talking to you! All you do is lie anyway! You're a liar; you always have been. You lied to get into this family. You lie to stay connected to it. You're the only one who doesn't belong and that makes you feel emasculated, so the only way to prove yourself worthy as a man is to use your dick. Well, that's not good enough, Gabriel Medlov. You're still a boy despite your best efforts. You're a boy dealing with grown men who see right through you. I see right through you, and I'm sick of it! You disgust me!!"

Gabriel couldn't take her words anymore. They were like nails digging down a chalk board. Feeling his anger boil to the very top, he drop the bag and turned to her.

"Well, what do you want to do then? *Huh?* You want to go?" he asked, screaming. "Go then, Briggy! It might be best for both of us. Just fucking go! I'll put you up somewhere. I'll pay for everything no different from what I'm fucking doing right now! So you can have the life you've always coveted."

"I do not covet," she snapped.

"You do not fool me. You don't think I know? I know you still think about fucking him, but it makes you feel better to have me around so that you can say that you have at least one Medlov, just not the one you want, because he would never marry you. You're just as weak as I am. But at least I have a birth right to be here and I'm not just holding on using my miserable fucking cunt! Just pack your things, find a map, pick a place and get out of my fucking life before you drive me insane!"

His words cut her deep. She had to look down just to make sure that she was not bleeding. "Yes," she croaked. "Yes, I want to fucking leave. I want to take me and my baby as far away from you as possible, because you are not worth it."

Gabriel's mouth flew open. She had just kicked the air right out of his diaphragm. Eyes narrowed, he shook his head. "You know, you really have the worst fucking timing I've ever seen in my life. You couldn't have just said that you were pregnant? You had to push me to say that shit to you so that you would feel better about leaving me?" His eyes gleamed with malice. "Well, good. Fucking great, Briggy. I hope that you got what you asked for." Tears fell down his cheeks. "I hope that I lived up to my father's standards for you. But at least when you're gone, you don't have to help carry around the shame that Anya could have very well been my *sister* if my father had gotten to Royal first, or that my cousin could have been fatherless for real if my father's attempts on Dmitry's life hadn't panned out. You have no idea what type of man it takes to stay here and face these people every single day, because you're too busy living the good life off my back."

He turned and headed toward the door. "Like I said, we'll talk when I return."

"I'll be gone when you get back," she warned, voice trembling.

Gabriel looked down at the floor, then turned slowly to her. His tone was different now. It was stern and direct. "No, you won't. You leave this house with *my child*, I'll find you. I swear. And I won't be forgiving about it. My mother did that to my father. *You know that.* And despite my shortcomings, you don't get to do that to me." He adjusted the bag on his large shoulder. "Now, we'll talk about this like adults when I get back. Then you can do whatever you want to do."

"I hate you!" she screamed. "I hate the day that I ever laid eyes on you!"

"Yeah, well get in line," he said, walking out of the door, and slamming it behind him.

Chapter 18

As quiet as a shadow, Vasily stood over Dylan watching him sleep peacefully, curled up to the new teddy bear that he had just bought him and holding on to the pillow for dear life. There was something so beautiful and unexplainable about the boy. But more than that, there was something incredible about how the boy made him feel inside. He gave him hope — pure, simple hope.

Vasily had to wonder if his own father ever once felt the way that he was feeling now, did he ever stare in awe of him, pray over him, did he worry about him? His father never outwardly showed any love toward him — not from the time that he was a baby until the day that he died, but now that Vasily was on the other side of the spectrum, he had to wonder.

Regardless of the answer being yes or no, Vasily did. He worried. He prayed his sins would never be visited on his son and that all the days of his life he'd be healthy and happy.

Before Dylan, the only children he had ever cared for had been the Medlov children. Anya had been his pride and joy along with Maxim, Konstantin and Alexandria, but now he had his own child, and regardless of what the paternity test said, he'd always be just that.

In such a short period of time, they had become inseparable, but after tonight, Vasily was certain that one way or another, things would change.

Putting a note by the bed addressed to him, he bent over Dylan and kissed his forehead, then stealthily made his way out of the room.

Boris was waiting outside in the hallway for his boss. When Vasily emerged, he closed the door behind him and nodded. "Keep him safe while I'm gone."

"Sure thing, Boss," Boris said, walking with Vasily.

"Where are we?" He checked his watch. They would be leaving the property in 10 minutes.

"Everything is ready to go. Chicago is waiting on you. Grigory and his team will be at the airport when you arrive. He's got an address on Yakov."

"That was quick," Vasily said impressed.

"Da, it cost," Boris explained.

"In this life, everything costs something," Vasily said, hitting the stairs. "Is everyone else ready to go?"

"They are getting there," Boris said hesitantly. "When I went to get Gabriel, he was screaming at his girlfriend. It didn't sound good."

Vasily always insisted on a full report, especially on Gabriel, He still didn't fully trust the man. Considering Gabriel's background with law enforcement, Vasily always felt as though the new addition to the Medlov family was not exactly on board with the core business of weapons, precious gems trafficking and their secondary but profitable businesses of extortion and contract killing.

In the Medlov Crime Family's entire existence, not one person had ever turned state's evidence and lived to testify. However, Vasily felt as though, if anyone could pull it off, it would be Gabriel, all the more reason to keep a very close eye on him and all of his clandestine activities. While Gabriel normally prefaced his late night meetings as sexual romps with women associated with the family, Vasily often wondered if he used this as a cover to smuggle information about the family out of the house.

Now, with his son also very much a part of the Medlov family, Vasily felt it important to watch Gabriel even closer. After all, he did not have any children, a wife or family outside of the people in the house. Gabriel was a wild card, and it puzzled Vasily as to why Boss Dmitry did not see it.

However, he could always be wrong. After all, he was only human and an extremely untrusting human at that. For all he knew, Gabriel was just an asshole.

And because of that possibility, he never accused or led on that he was untrusting of the man.

When Vasily arrived downstairs, everyone was waiting in the foyer. It was odd, because normally, he was the first one to arrive. This was the first time in his career that he'd been the one to be waited on.

Gabriel was first to say something. "What took you so long? Everything okay?" he asked concerned.

Anatoly smirked. "Ignore him. He doesn't have kids," he said, as the butler opened the door for them.

Vasily was suddenly embarrassed. "Sorry, Boss. I just wanted to..."

Anatoly cut him off. "You don't owe me an explanation, brat. Let's just go. I fucking hate Chicago. I just want to go do what we have to do and get back."

"Why do you hate Chicago?" Gabriel asked, ignoring the very smug, considering the information that he'd just received, very untrue statement that Anatoly had just made about him not having children.

"I got into some shit there once. Hated it ever since," Anatoly scoffed. "Vasily, you remember that shit? What was her name?"

"Helga," Vasily answered absently.

"Murdering bitch," Anatoly said, walking out of the door with his bodyguards leading the way. "It took five bullets to put her down."

Gabriel's eye rose. He was fascinated by how his cousin talked about murder and death like other people talked about shopping and movies. To Anatoly, life was just one big observation that he rarely got off the deck to participate in. Yet, unlike him, Anatoly seemed to breeze through life. He was born to the right father, picked the right woman, had a perfect daughter and a pretty cushiony job as the second in-charge of the largest Russian mob syndicate in the world.

Figures, Gabriel thought to himself.

Chapter 19

With Maxim curled up in Dmitry's massive arms after having a late evening bottle, he sat in his study alone watching the monitors while listening to the jazz station on his surround sound stereo system. He watched Gabriel, Anatoly and Vasily converse in the foyer before leaving; checked the monitors to see if the guards were making their rounds and finally, checked the balances on his main bank accounts. Now, he was ready to begin his real work.

Somewhere between Gabriel fighting with Briggy; Renee and Anatoly making love, Dmitry found the number to their trusted doctor and called him for a late night visit. He would arrive in less than an hour to swab Dylan's mouth and rush the samples back to the lab to get a definite answer on his paternity. Additionally, he also called their new attorney, Lawrence Massey, to come over to the house and begin to earn his $40,000 a month retainer.

Nothing was ever easy.

Dmitry knew that from years of experience. While the Boys were still trying to figure out how to brush their teeth, he was making hits on major crime bosses and going to war with whole countries. It was because of his experience, and the many brushes with death over the years, that while Anatoly and Gabriel didn't seem concerned about going to Chicago, he knew there could always be danger lurking at every corner.

But there was something more.

Something didn't add up to Dmitry.

Before Vasily had left, he had printed out the email that was sent to Lilly by her babysitter. Several hours ago, Leo had been in Jackson, Mississippi. There was no way that he was going to stay there, and unless he let on to knowing more than they thought, Leo had no idea that everyone was in Chicago.

What Leo did know was that Vasily obviously was not dead.

The Vory v Zakone while international in scope was a small community. Surely in 10 years, Vasily's old boss had learned, especially while incarcerated, that his attempt to take his life had been thwarted and that he was now thriving with the biggest boss in the world. News like that and even rumors of the possibility would have traveled fast.

Taking all of that into consideration, Dmitry knew that Memphis was close in proximity to Jackson and that Leo's next visit would be to his doorstep.

It would have been easy to vocalize that, but Dmitry was a man who believed in his son and the other men in his family learning through trial and error, when possible.

So, he opted to stay, wait and deal with the man himself. Plus, someone had to keep an eye on his family and when it came to them, Dmitry didn't take any chances. Not anymore, especially not after all of the hell that they had been through in the past.

There were also other things on his mind. He had watched the boys, each one, very carefully and noticed the smallest things about them. Without knowing the entire story, he knew that something was wrong with Gabriel and he knew that Vasily was growing out of his job. Both of these issues would need to be addressed before they got out of hand.

To jump the gun, conversely, would be a mistake. So, he'd let it play out and see how it all ended.

Like clockwork, a black E-Class Mercedes pulled up to the front door, and a young black man jumped out in a three-piece suit with a leather satchel on his arm. Dmitry looked over at the crystal Tiffany clock on his desk and saw the time, 40 minutes, not an hour. Impressive.

Pouring a small glass of water, he pushed back in his chair as Maxim stirred. The boy's eyes flashed open and locked on his father for a moment. Cradling him closer, Dmitry began to rock in the chair just enough to put the baby back to sleep. "Shh, little king, get some rest," he said, kissing the crown of his son's head. He snuggled him closer, taking in the smell of lotion and baby powder. How he loved that fragrance. There was nothing more important to him than his children, which was why he felt the urgency to call Lawrence.

Within minutes, the phone vibrated on his table. Dmitry picked it up answered in a low baritone, "Da."

"Boss, your lawyer is here," Boris said, ignoring his own fatigue. "Do you want me to walk him back to your office?"

"Yeah, send him back," Dmitry said, hanging up the phone.

His deep voice was just enough to wake his son up again and the boy immediately began to cry. Standing up, he bounced him and walked around his study while he patted his back. "There, there," Dmitry cooed. "No need to fuss."

Walking him to the large bay windows that looked out over the grounds, he hit a light switch on the wall and lit up the backyard. "Look at that," Dmitry said, kissing the boy's fat cheeks. "Look at that pretty night."

The boy, as if he understood, stopped crying and looked out of the window and immediately stopped his pout.

Dmitry smiled. "First, you conquer your yard, then you conquer the world," he whispered to the boy. As playful as his voice was, he was very serious. He had high hopes for his children, Anatoly included, and he wanted most of all for them to know that there was nothing in this world that was unattainable.

Opening the door to the study, Boris led Lawrence inside and pointed to the sofa. "Sit there," he said, roughly. His clenched jaw gave proof to his growing resentment for the younger man.

Lawrence obediently sat down, although he bristled at the brute Russian's command. The two had never really cared for each other, for personal and very cosmetic reasons, but considering their boss, they suffered each other. The alternative was much too costly.

Dmitry turned and looked at his lawyer, Lawrence was only 31 years old, a former University of Memphis football player and all around playboy. He liked the man on many levels and saw his potential. And in Dmitry's eyes, potential was a currency that should never be underestimated.

"How are you tonight, Sir?" Lawrence asked, unbuttoning his suit jacket.

"Good," Dmitry said, feeling Maxim fret again. "How are you?"

"Life is great," Lawrence answered honestly. *How could it not be with his salary?* Dmitry had recruited him right from under the nose of the Department of Justice by making him an offer that he could not refuse. When Lawrence saw the number that Dmitry had written down on a piece of paper and slid across the table to him at Mother Russia during his lunch break one winter afternoon, he had gone in the next day and immediately gave his two weeks' notice to the United States Attorney General for Memphis district. Since then, he had been a loyal worker for Dmitry.

"I brought you here in the middle of the night to handle something critical for me," Dmitry said as the door opened again.

Royal walked in glancing over at Lawrence before looking at Dmitry and in doing so she knew that he was up to something. She nodded toward the lawyer and then went to get her son. "I'll take him, baby," she said, arms already outstretched.

Dmitry reached down and handed his wife the baby carefully. "Are you sure? I know that you are tired."

Royal smiled at his concern. Even after so many years, he was still very thoughtful. "Kon is asleep with Anya. I'll be fine, baby." She rose up on her tippy toes and kissed her husband on his soft lips, lingering on his taste. "See you in just a bit?" Her brown eyes flashed open at him.

He rubbed her cheek. "Of course. I just have a few things to handle and then I'll be up. I won't be long," he said, knowing that she wanted to make up for what happened earlier to him. And he intended to let her.

"I'll be waiting," she said, wrapping her arms tightly around their son. She turned, bouncing the baby and headed towards the door. "Good evening, Attorney Massey."

"Ma'am," Lawrence said, standing in her presence. He had always admired the mysterious Mrs. Medlov. She never looked him in the eye, and he never dared to do the same. It was almost as though she was royalty, and to some, he knew that she was. Yet, her striking beauty made men want to gawk, always draped in diamonds and so regal in her demeanor – a perfect match for the Czar of the Underworld.

As the door closed quietly behind Royal, Dmitry redirected his attention. He was anxious to get this done now and get back to his wife. "It seems that your experience with the Department of Justice will come in handy again this week." Walking back to his seat, he sat down. "Come over here and sit by me." He saw another car pulling up in the driveway. It was the family doctor arriving to swab Dylan's mouth.

Lawrence was quick to move. "How can I help, Sir?"

Dmitry twisted his lip and knitted his long fingers together. "Two things. Leo Rasputin and the matter of a certain illegitimate child."

Lawrence's brow rose. "Leo Rasputin, Sir?"

Dmitry smiled. "Yes. Have you heard of him?"

"Indeed I have. He has been on every channel in the country and every BOLO list that law enforcement agencies have released since his escape from Attica," Lawrence said, pulling out his laptop. He could tell that he would be there all night.

"So, we're on the same page," Dmitry said yawning. "I want you to find out what the price on Leo's head is, and then I want you to contact the SAC for the FBI in Chicago and Manhattan. We have..." He scratched his stubbly beard, "a somewhat viable relationship with both agencies."

Lawrence was not surprised at that comment. He opened his Apple Air and put in his password. "And what are we requesting from your contacts?"

"Cooperation," Dmitry said flatly.

Chapter 20

Vasily was tired of planes. He sat in his seat, looking out of the window, thinking about Lilly, and trying to wrap his mind around why she had chosen to do everything on her own, if she had nothing to hide. Unfortunately, his emotions were showing on his face, something that rarely happened to him, but normally, his life was not his own. It was full of other people's requests and needs. This time, now that the focus was on him, he didn't like it very much. It made him feel vulnerable, open and out of control. The idea made him more sympathetic to the men sitting across from him. He realized how Anatoly's life must have changed so dramatically with a wife and a child of his own to watch over now. And for Gabriel, he did feel some sort of sympathy for him being the focus of every conversation about his father and his previous life as an agent.

Vasily liked being invisible. He liked being a fixture in the family without ever feeling or being made to verbalize anything outside of the Vory v Zakone.

Now, he was ... human.

Anatoly watched him without a word. Putting down his beer, he sat forward in the seat. "Brat," he said, with his arms resting on his denim covered.

Vasily looked over, "Da."

"It will be alright, you know."

Vasily smirked. "Easy for you to say. Renee has never stabbed you in the back."

Anatoly laughed. "Once they marry you, they stab you straight in the heart."

Vasily laughed a little, even though he didn't feel like it. "I keep..." he paused. Did he really want to open up the wound any farther?

"Go on, purge. You'll feel better," Anatoly said, unusually agreeable.

"Dr. Phil, maybe he doesn't feel like circle jerking at the moment," Gabriel sneered.

Anatoly turned to his cousin. "What the fuck is up with you?"

"Nothing," Gabriel said, resting back.

"Nothing my ass. You've been a dick the entire flight," Anatoly said, switching his attention. "What's going on with you? Briggy find out about another one of your pieces of non-descript ass?"

Gabriel rubbed his temples. "Since when did you become a fucking saint? You mean to tell me that you've never cheated on Renee?"

"No," Anatoly shrugged. "Is that so hard to understand?"

Gabriel sighed. "Whatever."

"What is it?" Anatoly pushed. "I know it's something."

"Briggy is pregnant," Gabriel finally said. "There...it's out there. She's pregnant and she wants out."

Anatoly and Vasily both looked over at Gabriel with a blank stare.

Vasily was actually glad that the focus had turned away from him, but the news was baffling.

Anatoly shook his head. "She knows too much to just get out," he said sternly. "What are you going to do?"

"I don't know," Gabriel said, rolling his eyes. "Pay for an abortion?"

Vasily looked at Anatoly. He knew that Dmitry would not approve.

"Do you want her?" Anatoly asked.

"No," Gabriel answered simply. "No, I don't want her and I don't want what you and Renee or, Dmitry and Royal or, even what Vasily and Lilly have. I don't fucking want any of it."

Anatoly picked his beer back up and sat back in the seat. "And that is why I gave up random ass," he joked.

"I'm not in the mood for you," Gabriel snapped. "You told me to be honest with her. Well, I was. I told her that I didn't love her, and that almost started World War III. She was livid with me."

"I know I told you to be honest with her, but do you really think tonight was the time?" Anatoly asked defensively. "What happened to you? You used to be the sensitive one."

"What happened to me?" Gabriel asked in a huff. "This life happened to me. I have random women thrown at me every time that I walk out of the door. I'm running guns and making deals in three different time zones daily. I'm stressed out and I'm realizing that if this is the life that I've chosen than monogamy is not an option."

Anatoly had felt that way before, so he could understand, but he really thought that

Gabriel had gotten used to things. "Do you feel any sympathy for Briggy? It's not her fault."

"You're right. It's not her fault," Gabriel admitted. "But it's the truth."

"You can't just cast her to the side. She knows too much," Anatoly reiterated. "You should have never fucked with her. Now, she's rolled into this family, and you can't just discard her, especially with a baby on the way."

"I don't want her to have an abortion. Let me just set the record straight, but I also don't want to be connected to that woman for the rest of my life." Gabriel buried his head in his hands. "Fuck. I'm screwed."

Vasily shook his head. Gabriel was cracking. He could handle leaving his job, handle facing his family, but he didn't do well with women at all.

"We'll talk about it once we get home," Anatoly said, pulling out his phone.

"What are you going to do, snitch to Dmitry?" Gabriel accused. Great. All he needed was another family meeting. For them to be organized crime leaders, they sure did feel like the 'Leave It To Beaver' clan.

"Do you really want one more woman running off tonight?" Anatoly asked, throwing up his hands. "Yes, I'm telling Papa to watch her. If you left her in the state that I think that you left her in, then she might already be gone."

That only made Gabriel feel worse. Suddenly, the attention was slowly moving back to him and his current situation.

Vasily laughed. *Life was a bitch*. "Women," he said, motioning for the stewardess. "Bring me a beer, please."

Anatoly couldn't help it. He laughed too. He winked at Vasily. "What did I tell you? In the fucking chest is where they stab you."

Texting his father, Anatoly looked over at Vasily. "Alright, you're next, purge."

"Oh, I don't have anything to say," Vasily said, unwilling to be as candid as Gabriel had been.

"You owe us, brat. We're on a plane chasing your old lady across the night. Now, what is the story?" Anatoly wouldn't take no for an answer.

"Yeah, you owe us. Join the ranks. Purge," Gabriel said, oddly feeling better.

"The whole story is short and simple. A little over 10 years ago, I worked for Leo Rasputin. He shot me when I tried to break up a fight between him and Lilly, who at the time was his girlfriend. He married her shortly after that."

"How shortly," Gabriel probed.

"About seven months after that, they got married."

"So seven months after he shot you, Lilly married him?" Gabriel said, flabbergasted.

"Yes, a few months after that, he was arrested and close to a year after I was shot, she testified against him. During that time, my friend, so I thought, called me and asked me to help her get out of Manhattan. I met him in Chicago and took her to Jackson, Mississippi."

"Why Jackson?" Gabriel asked.

"Yeah, why Jackson?" Anatoly asked also.

"Dmitry had sent me down there to buy up some storage space for guns that were being transported to New Orleans. It looked like a place that she would just blend in. There were plenty of Black people, not a lot of technology and not a lot of people who knew anything about Russian mobsters or their wives."

Gabriel twisted up his lip. "Yeah, I could see that."

"I'm glad that you approve," Vasily said, rolling his eyes.

"So, that accounts for one year. When did you knock her up?" Anatoly asked.

"Remember, I asked for a few days to get her situated?" Vasily said, seeing the Chicago skyline come into view from his window.

"Da, I remember. It was the only time you ever asked for time off."

"Well, I guess that's when I got her pregnant," Vasily said, looking at his watch.

"I can see why you never ask for time off," Gabriel joked. He raised his hands. "I'm fucking with you. Go on."

"It takes nine months to have a baby and Dylan is eight years and three months old." Vasily nodded. Yep. The math added up.

Anatoly huffed. "So, why don't you think the kid is yours? If the timeline adds up, then what other possibilities could there be?"

"She didn't call him my kid in the letter she left me. She called him her kid." Vasily's irritation began to show.

Anatoly smirked. "When Renee is mad at me, she calls Alexandria her daughter. It's a maternal thing. They take over all rights when they are pissed off. What else makes you think he's not yours?"

"Just a worry down in my gut," Vasily said, honestly.

"That's just worry." Anatoly shook his head. "Get used to the feeling. It never goes away. I'm always worried about the two of them. Every day, I'm fucking paranoid. And it was never like that before I got married. After Alexandria was born, my blood pressure shot through the roof."

"I guess that they are more worry than they are worth," Gabriel said absently.

Anatoly turned to his cousin. "No, cousin they are worth it. You just have to find the right one. And for the one that is on the way, you have to man up and be there for your child, regardless of how you feel about Briggy."

Gabriel's eyes locked on his cousin. "Yeah, I know." He sat back quietly. "I just … don't want to be the same let down that my father was. You know." He frowned. "I can't handle that shit."

"Gentlemen, we'll be landing in just a minute," the stewardess said, stepping out of the cockpit.

Chapter 21

By the time that Yakov's red eye plane arrived at Chicago's O'Hare International Airport, he was ready to pull his blonde hair right out of his head. Frustration had gripped him through the nerve-wrecking flight. Between his wife constantly worrying him about would they be okay and his son complaining about having to leave unexpectedly, he had all but gone crazy. In a rush, they had packed everything that they could fit in their bags, yanked them out of the trunk at La Guardia, drug them to the counter, checked them, thrown away bottles of his wife's unneeded lotions and perfumes, lost their son's ball and been forced to get rid of his flask under her jacket. On top of that, he was without a weapon, on the most dangerous trip that he'd ever taken his family on.

Quite simply, he wanted to scream.

As they exited the plane out into the swarms of busy people, he corralled his small family in front of him, looking around in every direction, trying to make sure that they were not being followed. He could not really be sure, though. There were way too many people and it seemed every other person looked Russian. His paranoia engulfed him.

When his wife accidently let go of his son's hand, he screamed at her.

"Hold on to him!" he had said, picking his son up and throwing him on his hip.

"I'm sorry," she said, tears in her eyes. "I'm trying as hard as I can, Yakov." Her tears and pleas fell on deaf ears that night.

Heart in his chest, he made his way to the baggage claim area where a large crowd of people waited. It seemed even with the long wait and delays, they were in a happy mood, moving as slow as possible and bringing him to a hot boiling rage.

He looked up at the monitors to see if their bags had been released and then back at his wife. "This is fucking ridiculous," he said, looking at his watch.

They had already arrived over an hour and half later because one of the key radar facilities was down due to a fire, now his bags were taking forever to get to him.

"Be patient, Yakov," his wife hissed. "You're driving me crazy, and you're scaring our son." She looked at the boy, who was confused by all of the ruckus.   "Maybe we should just go home."

"We can't go home," he said, looking back up at the monitor.   "We can never go home again until Leo is caught."   Shaking his head, he grabbed her arm.   "Forget this shit. I'll come back for it later. Right now, we have to go."

"What's left of my life is in that luggage," she complained. "Why can't we wait to get it?" She stalled, pulling away from him. Suddenly, none of this seemed like a good idea. She just wanted to go home to her family and forget the diamonds.

"No," he said, grabbing her again. "We have to go now."

Starting to pout, she finally followed him down the long terminal with hordes of people headed toward the rental cars.

As he passed a kiosk of cell phone accessories, a young man in jeans and a gray hoodie spotted him. He looked down at his cell phone to make sure he had the right man. Even though he'd never gotten a target wrong in the past, he couldn't make a mistake tonight of all nights. Sure that he had identified the right person, he waited a few seconds, put in his ear buds and then trailed a few feet behind the family.

He quickly sent a text to his boss.

He's here. Got a kid and a woman with him.

The text was quickly answered.

Take a pic. Follow close. Don't lose them.

Pavel did just as he was instructed. He took a picture of the three of them as they scurried quickly down the terminal, then went back to bobbing to his music, back pack thrown over his arm.

From the outside, Pavel looked like a regular teenager traveling alone, but actually he was a 20 year old runner for the Chicago branch of Dmitry's extensive family. When they got a call from the Medlov men in Memphis, everyone jumped to their jobs. It wasn't every day that the boss asked for a favor.

With sweat pouring down his face Yakov looked back, eyeing everyone. He immediately spotted Pavel, but couldn't be sure if the boy was a threat. The baby faced kid could have been just a traveler. There were at least a hundred like them passing by. Plus, in this day and age, no one wore visible tattoos anymore.

"We're getting a cab," Yakov said, changing directions.

"What about a car?" his wife said, confused.

"Fuck a car. We can catch a cab and be out of here quicker," Yakov said, moving his son to his other hip.

They headed toward the entrance, moving as quickly as their feet would take them. Pavel knew that he'd been spotted, so he put his phone up like he was talking as he passed Yakov.

"Did you see that motherfucker?," Pavel asked into a dead phone. "Man, I have never been able to wield a skateboard like that. I need to work on my skills." He made sure that Yakov heard him, and instantly he could see the man's shoulders begin to relax. "Dude, I'm going to catch a cab. Meet me at the Square for a beer before we go to Lena's house." Why he chose the name Lena, was beyond him, but he made it sound convincing.

"Daddy, I have to go pee," Yakov's son whined.

"Hold it," Yakov snapped.

"Yakov, he has to use the restroom," his wife said stopping. "Let me take him. You can't expect him to hold it all the way to where we are going, do you?"

Pavel slowed down but only a little. "Is Amy going to be there?" he asked, his American accent throwing Yakov off more.

Yakov eyed the boy, but when he kept going, he finally looked around for anyone else who might be suspicious. "Fine. I'll take him and then we go," he said, headed toward the restroom area.

**

Vasily, Gabriel and Anatoly sat with five of Dmitry's top men inside of Budem, a Russian restaurant in the heart of downtown Chicago waiting as they gave instruction to Pavel. On a struck of luck, they had been able to locate him with less trouble than they had first thought. All the planes coming from New York had been slowed due to an unrelated but fortunate event at the airport. It had allowed them to get their men in place. They had also sent men to the train stations, although they were sure that he would neither drive nor take a train because of his urgency to get out of Brighton Beach. Their calculations had paid off. Now, it was time to find out where he was going and make their final move.

Vasily looked at his watch again realizing that Lilly would be arriving in a few hours. He hoped by then to have Yakov neutralized and be able to move on to finding and stopping Leo once and for all.

Anatoly sat in the back of the fine dining restaurant, under dim lighting and fine china and quietly ate Ukrainian borscht while perusing the newspaper. Confident that his men would find Yakov, he had moved on to other business on his cell phone in between texting his wife and talking to Gabriel, who was still in a quiet uproar over Briggy.

Vasily felt more in his element now. He was doing what he was born to do -   Tracking, chasing, and ultimately, if he was really lucky, killing. One of the men brought him a gun case and set it quietly on the table in front of him. Vasily took his eyes off the front door for a moment and opened it.

Just what the doctor ordered.

"It's untraceable," Ruslan said proudly.

Vasily rubbed his hands over the guns quietly. *It's beautiful*, he thought to himself. He could feel the anxiousness coursing through him. He wanted … no at this point, want was such an inappropriate word … he needed to get this done. He pulled the twin Glocks from the case and held them up. They were the exact same size and color that Leo's man had used to shoot him in his back. He'd be happy to return the favor.

Ruslan checked his phone again. "They are on the move, Boss."

Vasily nodded. "Let me know when they arrive at their destination," he said, standing up. He walked outside in the night air and pulled out his phone. A picture of Dylan sitting in his bed with pajamas on was now his screen saver. He swiped the phone open and dialed Boris.

"Da, Boss," Boris answered on the first ring.

"Got any sleep yet?" Vasily asked.

"Not a wink" Boris said, watching the doctor load his small bag of equipment back into his car.

"How is Dylan?" Vasily asked.

"Went right back to sleep after the doctor swabbed his mouth. We told him that the doctor was checking him to see if he had strep throat."

Vasily was relieved. "So, it didn't scare him?"

"Nyet," Boris smiled. "He's a trooper. He barely moved."

"Do me a favor and make sure that he gets downstairs in the morning to get breakfast and that he brushes his teeth and puts on clean clothes. He doesn't always remember everything if you don't remind him." Vasily felt odd for sounding so paternal, but he wouldn't be able to focus if he didn't say something.

"He's taken care of, Boss. We're running a regular baby factory here. I know what to do," Boris assured him. "You find that bastard yet?"

Vasily looked back at the men circling around Anatoly at the back table of the restaurant. "Yeah, we've found him. Headed there now."

"Send a bullet for me," Boris said, headed back inside of the compound as the doctor drove away.

"Oh, I will, brat," Vasily said, hanging up the phone.

As he walked back inside, Anatoly stood up from the table and stretched. Slipping his gun holster on, he winked at Vasily. "We've got a tail on him. He's headed to Lincolnshire."

"Alright, everyone. Let's load up and head out. I want this fucker's head on a plate before dawn," Vasily said, going back to the table to retrieve his magazine clips.

Chapter 22

Yakov's tension began to subside as he and his family pulled up to his old condo off Rivershire Lane. A sight for sore eyes, it sat in the same state that he had left it. It was dark and quiet with only the street lights to illuminate the tree covered path. Bugs flew up into the halogen lamps and lightning bugs played around the rows of bushes up against the contemporary building. He quickly paid the cab driver and jumped out with his family. Digging in his pocket for the key, he walked along with his son on his shoulder sleeping and his wife dragging slowly behind up to the front door. Putting in his code, he heard the door unlock and as it swung open, cold air rushed over him, cooling his burning body.

Muriel looked up at him with a look of desperation in her eyes. *Were they finally here?* It felt like it had taken forever. She followed him through the quiet lobby to the bank of elevators and waited as the bell rang and the lift opened.

They loaded in quietly, drained of words.

A short minute later, they were on the eighth floor.

He led them to the condo that he had kept to himself as his own personal secret for over a decade. Slipping the key into the lock, felt like freedom. He opened the door and stepped inside.

Everything was as he had left it.

"How did it stay so clean?" Muriel asked. True the furniture was dated, but everything was clean and quiet.

"I paid the neighbor," he said, closing the door behind him.

"All this time?" she asked, frowning.

As he turned on a lamp in the small living room, he passed her their sleeping son. "Let me check everything." He walked through the small condo, turning on each light, checking in the closets and under the bed, pulling at the windows and looking for anything that might be out of place. "All clear." He waited as Muriel walked into the small guest bedroom.

She looked around approvingly. "So is this our new home?" she asked.

"Only for a while." He walked over and kissed her on her forehead. "Everything will be alright. Trust me."

She tried to smile back, to provide him with that vote of confidence that he surely needed. "I do trust you," she said, resting her head on his rock hard chest.

He took his son and laid him in the bed. Pulling his shoes off of him, he slipped the covers over his body and stood over him. "I'm going to provide the life for him that I never had."

The promise made Muriel's heart began to beat slowly again. It was his confidence that had sold her on this pipe dream, and she needed him to have that same confidence now to see them through.

Grabbing her by her small hand, he led her out of the room and closed the door. "I've got to call my contact tonight. It's imperative that we move these diamonds by tomorrow and get ready to leave the country."

She yawned but agreed. "Do you have any-one in mind?"

"Yeah." He took a seat on the leather sofa and patted the place beside him for her to sit down. "I know a guy. I'll call him and get things in order. You should try to get some rest now."

She sat beside him and melted into his large body. Resting her head on him, she listened to his heartbeat. "Yakov, are we going to get that woman killed?"

Yakov took Muriel's face in his hands. "My only job is to watch out for you and Stepan. Lilly made her bed. Let her lay in it, da."

She nodded. "It just feels wrong, is all."

"Life is wrong," he said, pulling out his cell. "I better get on this." Standing up, he passed her the remote. "Watch some television. Watch a DVD," he chuckled, "or a video cassette." There was a massive collection of dated movie tapes and more modern DVDs waiting for her to pick from.

She laughed, lightening the mood. "Wow, it's like walking into history," she said, getting up to take a closer look at his collection in the entertainment center across the room.

Yakov walked to the door of the master bedroom and looked in. "I'm scared to see what type of clothes I have in there, but they'll have to do. There is a washer next to the kitchen. You can wash your clothes and Stepan's. While I'm out tomorrow, I'll pick up something for you and maybe stop back by the airport."

"That would be great," she said. "Right now, I'm starving. I don't suppose that you have something in the fridge?"

"Afraid not," he said, fishing through the mail in a milk crate by the garbage can. "I'm sure there is a pizza place open around here. Why don't you just order something, but pay with cash?" He pulled out a wad of hundred dollar bills and passed her several twenties, then passed her a pizza ad. "Will you be okay, while I take care of this?"

She took the piece of paper from him. "I'll be fine," she said, looking around the room again. "Go on, baby. Do what you have to do. I can handle the house stuff."

Yakov walked over and kissed her again. This time on the mouth. It was a slow, sensual kiss, the same type that had stolen her heart. He knew that he had been a complete asshole for a couple of hours and now sincerely regretted it. "I love you," he whispered.

"I love you," she whispered.

***

The convoy of SUVs could not be mistaken as they trailed up the quiet lane toward Yakov's condo. In each vehicle one Medlov sat surrounded by a truck full of Chicago gangsters, strapped and ready to destroy. For them, this event was on a timer. They knew that they could not be in the city for long, and they knew that they had more than one object. With time of the essence, everything had to play out right.

As they pulled up in front of the building, the men jumped out and headed straight for the front door. A couple was headed back in from a date and had just put their code into the security system when Ruslan, a tall, broad man with so many tattoos on his body until he looked like a circus freak, stepped in front and grabbed the door. His very appearance startled them into shock. Black as night eyes. Black as night hair. Full pink lips and dark tan skin.

"After you," he said, as they quickly rushed inside.

He held the door as nearly 15 men strode inside, then closed it carefully behind him.

The doorman, who had been asleep for nearly two hours, quickly woke up. He stood rigid behind the desk as Vasily approached. He tried to straighten his ridiculous uniform to no avail. Wiping a hand over his balding head, he cleared his throat.

"I'm looking for this man," Vasily said, sliding his phone across the marble top. He eyed the man as he looked at it.

He shook his head. "I'm not supposed to give out..."

Vasily cut him off with a dismissive wave. "Do you want our next visit to be to your home? Maybe to your mother's home?"

The man shook his head emphatically.

"Then where's this guy?" Vasily urged.

"I don't know," the man answered sincerely. "I've been asleep, sir."

"Figures. Do you have a surveillance camera around here?" Gabriel asked.

The man moved back from the view of the cameras so that Gabriel could see.

"Rewind it and find him," Vasily ordered.

Five minutes later, they watched Yakov enter the building on the camera system.

"Eighth floor," the man croaked. "Apartment 815."

"Now, was that hard?" Gabriel asked, hitting the man on the head. "Call the police and it will be your last neighborhood watch. Got it chief?"

"Got it," the man answered, looking around at the lobby full of men. There was no way that he wanted to get caught in this shit storm.

"Three stay here with Mr. Belvedere, three take the stairs, six take the elevators," Vasily said, headed toward the elevators himself.

The men all took their positions or headed to their destination while Vasily entered the elevators with Gabriel and Anatoly along with three other men. Cocking his gun Vasily stilled his disposition.

Anatoly pulled out his cell phone.

"Really?" Gabriel asked.

"It's Papa," Anatoly said, reading the text. He sighed and raised a brow. "We have to make sure that the diamonds are there before we kill him."

"What?" Gabriel said, rolling his eyes. "Why?"

"That's what the fucking man just said." He showed him his phone. "Don't kill him unless the diamonds are there. See, it says it right there."

"Well," Vasily said, cocking his gun. "Let's hope that the diamonds are there."

As the doors to the elevator opened, they carefully exited, seeing their men meet them at the emergency exit. They slowly made their way down to Yakov's door.

Standing on either side of the door, they waited as one of the men knocked on the door.

Muriel was sitting in the living room watching television while Yakov took a shower. "That was fast," she said, looking at the clock. Grabbing the money off the end table, she walked to the door. "Coming," she called out.

Yakov heard the door, from the shower and turned off the water. Looking at his watch, his heart dropped. It would take a pizza guy a hell of a lot longer than that to deliver food. "Muriel, don't answer it!" he screamed as he jumped out of the shower and ran for the door naked.

It was too late.

As soon as Muriel opened the door, the man on the other side pointed the gun at her and pushed her back inside of the apartment. Screaming, she fell back on the floor, moving away from him.

Yakov came barreling out of the bedroom toward her and ran directly into Vasily. His feet halted on the carpet as he looked at his wife, being held at gun point. Vasily took one look at him and punched him dead in the nose. Blood flew against the wall and Yakov fell backwards.

"Stand up, you piece of shit!" Vasily ordered.

Yakov stood up and grabbed his broken nose. Blood dripped down his chest and pooled down his abdomen.

Vasily put his hands over his lips and looked at Muriel. "Shh," he said, gun pointed. "Take her over to the couch."

"Don't hurt her. She has nothing to do with this," Yakov begged. He looked toward the door on the other side of the living room in desperation.

Vasily trailed his gaze to the door and walked toward it.

"Wait," Yakov said, hands raised. His hairy, blonde chest expanded in fear. He forgot that he was uncovered.

"Can someone give him a towel?" Anatoly said, walking casually over to the bar connected to the small kitchen.

"What is all of this about, Vasily?" Yakov asked, trying to keep him away from his son's room. "What do you want?"

Vasily walked to the bedroom door and opened it. Looking in on the small boy, he shook his head and closed the door again. "Where are the diamonds, Yakov?" His deep baritone echoed across the room.

"I don't know what you're talking about," Yakov lied as Muriel sobbed.

Vasily looked over at Muriel. "Is it worth it to lose your life trying to protect something that isn't even rightfully yours?" he asked.

She shook her head, eyes blood shot red. Trembling, she begged. "Please don't hurt my son."

"I'm not here for your son. I'm not here for you. I'm here for Yakov and the diamonds," Vasily answered flatly. "Take the gun from her head. She can't think with that thing pointed at her."

Anatoly didn't flinch. This was Vasily's show. He was just an observer for the moment, besides, he knew that the man would never hurt Muriel or the kid in the next room. But he would make her watch her husband be tortured if it meant getting what they came for.

When the gun was removed from her temple by one of Dmitry's soldiers, she nearly collapsed against the couch. "Please," she begged. "Leave us alone."

"Just tell me where the diamonds are," Vasily said, voice raising in irritation.

Still Muriel said nothing. Instead, she looked over at her husband.

"We don't have all night," Anatoly reminded.

"Let's start with a question that you can answer then," Vasily said, walking up to Yakov, who was still standing with hands in the air. He looked the man in the eyes as he stood butt naked. "When did you fuck Lilly?"

Yakov frowned. "I didn't..."

Vasily put the gun to Yakov's head and drew the hammer back.   "Do you think that I'm fucking with you? Do you think that I came all the way just to fuck with you?"

"No!" Yakov screamed as the cold steel pushed against his temple. "I didn't fuck her! I swear!"

Muriel's face went pale. "What?"

"I didn't," Yakov said again as he shrunk from the weapon. "We stopped. Okay. The agent came back to the door to check on her and we stopped. I took the diamonds and I left. I never..." He shook his head. His voice leveled out as he looked at Vasily. "I never fucked her. I swear it."

"One bit of good news," Gabriel said, leaning against the door.

"But then you told Leo that she had the diamonds when he came to you the other day," Vasily said, grabbing him by his blonde locks. He drug him into the middle of the room and threw him on the floor, emasculated in front of his wife.

"We had a deal. She got out of Manhattan and I got the diamonds.   That was the deal. Yes, I told Leo that she had them, but I just assumed that you would keep her safe and no one would be the wiser. It wasn't like he was going to come for you knowing that you worked for Dmitry Medlov," Yakov explained quickly.

"Can someone please get him a fucking towel," Anatoly said, turning around. "I don't care to see his dick slinging around all night."

One of the men darted in the bedroom and brought back a towel. He threw it over to Yakov. "Suka," the man murmured.

"So, we are back to the first question," Gabriel said, walking closer. "Where are the diamonds?" He stood over the man with his gun at his side, tapping his thigh. Looking over at Muriel, he asked her, "Do you know."

"Just tell him, Yakov," Muriel begged.

Vasily bent to him and looked him in the eye. "You were supposed to be my brat. And you sold me out. You watched me get shot. You tried to fuck Lilly and then you basically put a hit on her when you lied so that you could run off with your wife, your kid and the diamonds. You're a real low life piece of shit. You know that?"

"I sold out Lilly. What the fuck difference does it make? She's just some fucking bitch from Harlem. She's not worth the trouble," Yakov said, spitting blood. He shook his head. "What does it matter to you?"

"You're not the only one with a son," Vasily whispered.

Yakov looked up. "With her?" Suddenly, the theatrics made sense. He dipped his head in shame.

"Did you fuck her?" Vasily asked again.

Yakov paused and looked in between his wife and the men. "No," he said, clenching his aching jaw.

Anatoly's phone rang. He answered it quickly. Looking over at Vasily, he whirled his finger around and hung up the phone. "Let's wrap this shit up. Police are on the way."

"Take the woman in the room with the kid," Vasily ordered.

"No," Yakov screamed, fighting to get back up. "Don't hurt my fucking family. I'll tell you where they are. Just don't hurt them."

The men were obedient to only one voice. They drug Muriel screaming and kicking out of the living room. "I love you!" she cried. "Ya-kov!!!"

"Please!" Yakov fought to get up off the floor. "I'll tell you anything. Don't kill my family."

Vasily had no intention of doing so, but he didn't tell Yakov that. "Where are they?" he asked.

"Behind the entertainment center. In the back of the fucking television," Yakov screamed. "They are right there." He pointed at the old system.

Vasily nodded at the men. "Get them."

They quickly knocked the system over on the floor. Video cassettes and DVD flew across the room. Kicking in the back of the older floor model 60 inch television, the found a box of diamonds. They opened it and brought it over to Vasily.

"Check them," he said, passing them to An-atoly.

He took and look and nodded. "They are the real thing. It's about $20 million worth."

"Now, you have what you came for. Please leave my family alone," Yakov begged. "Don't let them hurt my boy."

"We're not going to hurt your boy," Vasily said, standing over Yakov. "But I am going to let you see this coming." Pulling back the trigger, he shot Yakov point blank in the shoulder and leg.

Anatoly laid the diamonds out on the counter.

"What are you doing?" Gabriel asked.

"Papa said to leave them. There would be someone to pick them up," Anatoly answered.

"Who?" Gabriel asked, frustrated.

"The Feds," Anatoly said, looking at his phone. "Lilly called the fucking Feds about the diamonds. We're supposed to leave him here with them."

"Alive?" Gabriel said, throwing up his hands.

"Yes, fucking alive," Anatoly said, walking out of the door.

Vasily kept his gun pointed on Yakov, wanting to kill him more than anything. "The only reason that you aren't dead, is because you didn't leave me that way. But rest assured when you get out of prison, if you dare think about coming to find Lilly, I'll finish what I started."

"He's been warned. Let's go," Anatoly called out from the hallway.

Leaving Muriel and her son locked in the bedroom, the men exited quickly.

As they got back into the elevator, Anatoly looked over at Vasily. "You did well."

"Fuck that," Vasily said, hitting the side of the elevator. "I should have killed him."

"No, you wanted to kill him. But you're not the boss. Papa says let him live, we let him live. Besides, your girl made a deal, and it doesn't work without all of the pieces."

Vasily shook his head in disbelief. All of this for nothing. "Is she here in Chicago?"

"Arriving soon." Anatoly tapped him on the shoulder. "There are plenty of people to still kill," he said reminding him of Leo.

Chapter 23

As the sunlight crashed into the small room, Lilly woke up from her sleep to find that she was in Chicago. The train had come to a stop and she was finally at her destination. Pulling herself out the ball that she had curled up in on the cot, she sat up on the side and wiped her face. A nervous pang ripped through her at the thought of all that she had to try to do to keep her family safe, but she was more than willing. Besides, she was here now. There was no way to back out.

Grabbing her phone, she looked down at the screen and saw that it had gone dead.

"No," she said, nearly crying. "No, no." She picked the phone up and clutched in in her hands as she bent over and let out a groan. How was Agent Sheldon supposed to reach her now?

Rocking, she closed her eyes tight and bit down on her dry lips. A tear escaped, despite her best efforts to keep it at bay. "Lord," she prayed. "Please Father, help me."

She was so afraid. She felt so damned alone.

Standing up on shaky legs, she grabbed her bag and opened the door to her small compartment. People laughed and talked as they moved past her. For just a moment, she was envious of them, until she thought of Dylan waiting for her back in Memphis.

No, she wasn't alone.

She was needed. She *had* to do this.

Wiping her eyes, she stepped out among the people and followed everyone as they exited off the train out into the terminal.

Looking for the exit, she headed toward the signs that led her out to the street. First thing first, she had to charge the phone and get to Sheldon, then she had to find her way back to Yakov's apartment.

It has been a long time, but she still remembered two things. Lincolnshire and Rivershire. That location was the key to her salvation. And no matter what she wouldn't leave until she handed Yakov and the diamonds over to the FBI. No more would she allow her past to cloud her future. And no more would she allow those men to bully her.

Even if it killed her, she would stand up to them today.

Pulling her baseball camp down over her weary eyes, she walked out onto the streets of Chicago. The bustling city was busy with cars and people moving at warp speed. She had forgotten just how busy a city could be. Jackson was sleepy and slow and outside of a brisk walk down Main Street, she had never really seen Memphis. Though if she ever made it out of this, she promised to finally take Dylan on that trip and she planned to not to work so hard that she missed everything that made life sweet.

As she was about to hail a taxi, a hand gripped her arm and pulled her away from the edge of the street.

Looking back with adrenaline raging, she was shocked to see Vasily.

He stood there looking like Christmas morning. His green eyes burned through her with passion that she didn't believe that she'd ever seen before. He was absolutely breathtaking in his jeans and t-shirt, looking like a normal guy. Muscles ripped out of his cotton t-shirt. His arms bulged with tattoos. She looked at him and saw him possibly for the first time in her life.

This was the man that she was willing to give everything for.

And it was worth it.

Her eyes immediately welded up with tears. Whirling around, she grabbed him and hugged him tight. "Vasily," she said, trembling. "Oh my God. How did you know?" Her face was warm now, covered in tears of both happiness and sorrow.

The sunlight danced off her beautiful face. "What are you doing?" Vasily asked, rubbing her cheeks. "Why did you leave me?" He forgot his normally chilly disposition and relished the moment.

She looked at him with shock. "I wasn't leaving you. I was trying to stay with you forever," she said, voice quivering. "I was trying to make this right. It was my fault. I got you shot once, I wasn't about to risk your life again. I couldn't bear it. I knew that you'd take care of Dylan. I knew that you'd see to him being happy."

Vasily buried his face into her hair and held her. "I thought that you had left me again to run off and..." He could not bring himself to say it now that he knew that truth. He had judged her so wrongly, but never again.

"No," Lilly cried. She took in the smell of his cologne and rubbed his back. Swallowing hard, she released her words in his ear. "I love you."

Just as she said the words, he raised up and looked at her. His face was no longer stoic. Studying her every feature, he smirked. "I love you both." Looking up at the sky to keep showing to much emotion all at once, he let go of a sigh. "I can't lose you again. I can't go through it. I realized that the moment that I thought that I'd lost you."

"I have to do this," she said, shaking her head. "I made a deal."

"I know."

"No, you don't." She looked out at the street, debating what to do now. "I have to deliver Yakov and the diamonds, and if I can, I have to deliver Leo too. I don't know how, but it's got to be done or this will never end."

Vasily touched her cheeks again. For her to be so little, she was so brave. He nodded. "It's done."

"What?" she asked confused.

He shrugged. "It's done. The diamonds and Yakov. It's done. Sheldon has both."

"What? How?" she said, stepping back. Her brow furrowed. "I don't understand."

"You don't have to understand as long as you trust me. Do you?" Vasily waited.

Lilly nodded. "Of course, I trust you, Vasily. You're the father my child." She wiped another tear and nodded. "I trust you."

Vasily smiled. "Da."

"Da," she said, hugging him again.

"Good. Then let's go home," he said, pointing down the curb to the black Yukon waiting on them.

Anatoly stuck his head out of the door, dawning a pair of Aviator shades with his ear pressed to the phone and smiled. "Let's go. My folks are tired of babysitting your brat."

Chapter 24

Dmitry was never a late sleeper, but today, he moved with purpose. After breakfast with the family, Dylan included, he headed with his men to Mother Russia. It was an unusually short drive this morning, most because he was eager to arrive.

As they arrived downtown, he gave his driver different instructions from normal. "Park out front," he said, sitting in the passenger seat.

"Out front, Boss?" his driver asked.

"Da, you know where that is?" Dmitry asked with a crooked grin on his face.

"Yes, Sir," he said, pulling up to the front of the restaurant. Dmitry stepped out of the white Bentley into the sunlight and looked around.

The hostesses saw him and immediately opened the doors. He breezed through with a hello, paper under his large arm and shades covering his ice blue eyes.

"Is there something wrong, sir?" the manager said, running from the back.

"No," Dmitry said, looking at his watch. "How long has the truck outside across the street been there?"

"An hour," the woman answered, looking out of the bay windows.

"Boris," Dmitry said, headed to one of the private rooms in the back.

"Yes, Boss," Boris said, walking behind him.

"Invite our guests in and put out something to eat, ladies," he said, opening the Tiffany glass covered French doors to the back. "Don't bother patting them down."

Boris turned on his heels and headed back in the direction that he had come.

Everyone scurried, except Dmitry, who took his time. He sat down at the head of the long wooden table and laid out his newspaper. *Business section first, crime second.*

"Would you like some coffee?" one of the waitresses asked, rushing into the room.

"That would be lovely, Anjelica. Thank you," Dmitry said, taking off his shades. He ran his fingers down the bridge of his nose and pulled out his glasses.

As he did, he heard a borage of footsteps on the hardwood floor, headed toward him. Boris was the first to appear in the room. "Boss, you've got company. Leo Rasputin wants to have a word with you," he said, voice tight.

"Invite him in," Dmitry said, not bothering to look up from his paper. He wasn't about to give these yahoos that much respect. They didn't deserve it.

Leo and Taras walked in with several men behind him. Dmitry ran his hand over the table and smoothed out his paper. "Gentlemen. Have a seat," he said, softly. "Your other men can wait outside. Boris will tend to them."

Taking a seat at the other end of the table, Leo looked down at Dmitry and clucked his tongue against the bridge of his mouth. "Nice place ... Boss."

"Thank you," Dmitry said, slowing looking up at him. He detested insolence, especially from a man so insignificant. "How can I help you?"

Dmitry's glare made Leo's eye twitch. "I came to talk to you about one of your men."

"Which one?" Dmitry asked, turning the page to his newspaper. "I have many."

"Your right hand, Vasily." Leo tried to maintain eye contact though it was getting harder by the moment. But there was no way that he could punk out in front of his men.

"What about him?" Dmitry asked as the waitress brought him his coffee. She set it beside him and looked down at Leo. "Can I offer you something to eat or drink, sir?"

"Anything you have would be great. I'm fucking starving," Leo said, looking around the restaurant. "Coffee to start ... please," he said, sucking his teeth.

Dmitry nodded at Anjelica. "Coffee will be fine for now," he said, smiling at her.

Anjelica nodded and quietly excused herself, closing the doors behind her.

"You were saying," Dmitry continued. He sat up straight, showing his height more as his body went rigid. He glanced over at Taras, who stepped back into the shadows of the room out of the view of Dmitry.

"Vasily was one of my men. He crossed me over my wife and I shot him."

"I heard," Dmitry said, tilting his head. "But she wasn't your wife at the time."

"She became my wife."

"Interesting."

"Anyway, after my trial, my *wife* testified against me and ran off with $20 million in diamonds. My diamonds. And I think that she ran into the arms of your man, Vasily. I thought you'd want to know that about someone on your payroll."

"$20 million is not a lot of money," Dmitry said, sipping his coffee. "Not to me."

"Well, to Vasily and Lilly, it's a hell of a lot of money. The code says..."

"Are you really here to recite my law to me?" Dmitry asked, eyes narrowing.

"I'm here to ask you to hand him over," Leo said, correcting himself. "I know that you are a man who believes in standing by our principles."

"And your principles include shooting a man in the back and chasing a woman around the United States, putting her life in peril over something that you're not absolutely sure that she has?"

"Oh, the bitch has them," Leo pushed.

"I'm afraid not.   Your friend Yakov has them," Dmitry said with a smile.   "He was apprehended this morning in Chicago. I think he has to be patched up a little, but he's headed to prison.   The diamonds are headed to their rightful owner and you are on a wild goose chase. I'm sorry my friend. You have been led astray."

The discomfort was visible on Leo's face. He pushed his arms out on the table and shook his head. "She set him up."

"Lilly set him up?" Dmitry asked, amused.

"Yes, that bitch, set him up. Yakov would never..."

Dmitry had heard enough. "Don't be so blind. Of course, Yakov took the money. He tried to fuck your wife and he ran off with your diamonds." He didn't blink. Staring at the man, he waited for Leo to respond.

"So, I'm supposed to walk away with nothing?" Leo asked.   "I'm just supposed to take this shit?"

Dmitry chuckled. "Such is life. Full of surprises, isn't it?"

"Where is she?" Leo asked. "She's my wife. She belongs to me."

"She divorced you." Dmitry took another sip of his coffee.

"She belongs to me," Leo said again.

Dmitry said nothing.

"Well, I guess we are done here," Leo said, standing up. "Thank you for nothing."

"Are you not going to enjoy a little something to eat before you get back on the road?" Dmitry asked.

"No," Leo said, snarling. "I don't think that I want to dine with you. You'll forgive my rudeness, but I think that I've lost my appetite."

"Before you go, I think that you'll find one something very interesting," Dmitry said, standing up.

Leo looked up at the giant man in amazement but tried to hide it. "What's that?"

"There is a $1 million reward on your head. Dead or alive," Dmitry said, slipping his hands in his pockets.

"What's a $1 million to a man like you?" Leo clenched his fists.

"To me," Dmitry smiled. "To me $1 million is nothing, but to your men ..." Dmitry looked out the glass at the briefcase being set in front of them by Dmitry, "to your men, it's a lot of money."

Taras was the first to react. Pulling out his weapon, he took one look at Dmitry and shot Leo in the back before he could reach for his own gun. His body flew forward against the table. Shooting him again, Taras stepped closer and shot him again. This time in the head. Brain matter splashed across the room, barely missing Dmitry's white linen shirt.

"And that my friend is what getting shot in the back feels like," Dmitry said, looking over at his stained newspaper. *Pity.*

He stepped back and nodded at Taras in approval. "Collect your man and your money and be gone before it's time to open for lunch," he said, opening the doors to the room.

"Yes, Sir."

Leo's other men looked up stunned but relieved. They had a cut of the money, but had little work to do.

Walking past the men, Dmitry headed to the door where Boris and his men were waiting.

"I don't recall giving them my word. Did you?" Dmitry asked under his breath.

"No sir. I just explained what the money was for," Boris answered.

"Good, because I'd hate to go back on my word and be a liar. Let them collect Leo and the money and then get rid of them somewhere away from my restaurant. And Boris, bring back my million dollars, eh?" Dmitry hit Boris on the shoulder, sure that he would carry out his orders down to the last detail.

"Yes, sir," Boris said, looking back at the greedy traitors as they collected their bounty.

Anjelica came around the corner with a bag of cleaning supplies. "Should I keep the restaurant closed for the day, sir?" she asked unmoved by the scene.

"No dear, please open on time," Dmitry said with a smile as he walked back out into the sun.

It was a beautiful day. Suddenly, he felt like a stroll.

Chapter 25

When the car pulled around to the front of the Medlov Compound after their long travel, Lilly had never seen anything more beautiful than the sight of the regal mansion in front of her.

Before the driver could open the door good, she rushed out of the car and ran into the house, straight for Dylan. He was downstairs playing pirates again, and quietly waiting for his mother to return.

She dropped to her knees and held him close. His smell was intoxicating. Hugging and kissing him, knowing that he was completely oblivious to what had transpired over the last day, she relished in the moment for a second chance. She kissed him for everything that they had gone through and everything that they never would go through again.

In complete satisfaction everyone watched, even Gabriel and Briggy who stood on opposite sides of the living room. He had smiled at her, despite the situation, realizing for the first time in a long while, how important family was, not just to everyone else, but to him.

Shortly after their arrival, Dmitry had also come in. Anya was there playing with Dylan, but as usual; as soon as she saw her Daddy she jumped into his arms and began to kiss him.

Without saying a word, she had known the entire time that something was wrong. She had a knack for eavesdropping and had heard some of the gossip. Yet, like a good girl, she kept her mouth closed, and waited for everything to work itself out.

Dylan lit up when Vasily came sluggishly through the door. Pulling away from his mother, he ran to him and held on to his legs.

"I'm glad you're home," Dylan said, deaf to his innocent omission.

Vasily reached down and picked him up. "I'm glad to be home," he said, hugging him. "I missed you."

"I missed you, too," Dylan said, pulling at his dog chain. "Now that you're home, can we have that conversation?"

Vasily chuckled and set him down. "That's exactly what I had in mind. Want to talk about it over breakfast?"

"I ate with everyone else, but I could go for some orange juice," Dylan said in his most grown up voice.

"Great, I love orange juice," Vasily said, looking over at Lilly. "Let's go have that talk. Momma, are you coming?"

Lilly wiped her face and stood up from her crouched position. "Yes," she said, knowing what Vasily was about to tell him.

***

Sitting around the kitchen table together, Vasily looked over at Dylan and felt a complete spiritual connection to the boy. There was no doubt that he was his son, especially since he now knew the truth about Yakov.

Vasily reached over and pulled Dylan's chair closer to him. Rubbing through his curly locks, he smiled, trying to suppress rising nervousness. "Do you know why I'm proud of you?" he asked.

Dylan looked surprised. "You're proud of me?" A silent glee permeated the boy's smile.

Vasily frowned, shocked that Dylan didn't already know that. "I'm very proud of you."

"Why?" Dylan asked, both hands around the large glass of orange juice. He took another gulp of the orange juice, a testament to his truth, that he loved the beverage.

"Because you," Vasily lifted his chin, so that his son could see his eyes, "are the very best of me."

Lilly ducked her head. The sight was almost more than she could take, yet everything that she had wished for. Still, it would have been off-putting to cry in front of Dylan at the moment.

"The very best of you?" Dylan put down his glass. "What do you mean?"

Vasily's mouth curled at the corners. "I mean that you make me proud to be your father, and as my son, you make me complete." He was unapologetic in his words and sincere in their meaning.

Dylan couldn't help but smile. "Are you saying that you're my daddy?" He looked over at his mother, who nodded reassuringly.

"Da, da, boy. I'm your father," Vasily said, hoping that Dylan would approve.

Scooting out of his chair, Dylan dove into his father's arms again.. "That's the best news ever." Hugging him tightly, he laughed, lighting up the room with joy.

"I'm glad that you think so; I'm relieved actually." Vasily pulled at his chin.

Lilly couldn't help it now as large tears rolled down her cheeks.

"So I get to call you Dad?" Dylan asked, sitting on his lap.

"You do," Vasily said with a grin.

"And do we get to do father and son stuff like other boys?" Dylan asked.

"We do," Vasily answered.

"And are you going to marry mom?" Dylan asked, looking back at Lilly. "Because I don't just need a dad. She needs a husband. And we're sort of a package deal."

Lilly began to blush. She was just about to cut him off before Dylan could embarrass her anymore but Vasily answered.

"I am," he said, looking across at her. "One day. If she'll have me."

Lilly nodded, jaw jutted. "I will."

Epilogue

When Lilly got to her bedroom, she couldn't stand waiting any longer. Tearing out of her clothes, she fell into bed with Vasily, glad to finally be alone with him.

Her heart lurched as he peeled out of his clothes, one hypnotic layer at a time. His finely formed body flexed with want as he walked over to her and picked her up off the floor.

"Damn it, I'm missed you," he said, pulling her head to him.

His kisses were deeper than before. Not able to get close enough, she clung to him, melted into him. He rubbed her body all over, kissing every crease, sucking every tip, until she was ripe and begging for his entry.

Finding her core, he pushed into her body and felt her blossom. His domineering hunger made her quickly acquiesce to his pleasures. Arching her back, she gripped his body and took all of him into her, free from worry, free from guilt.

Whispers between them were sweet and full of love and promises. She couldn't help the feeling of pure excitement that rose in her. She was finally his. And he was finally hers.

They moved as if to a melody in the bed, dancing about the positions like partners in a waltz. These were the treasured moments that they had both been denied throughout their life. This was the connection that they had never had before and now that they had finally found each other, it was perfect.

Kissing her eyes Vasily held her close as he rocked inside of her body. His strong thighs parted, he found his home somewhere between her womb and her heart.

In perfect synchronicity they found their release, but only for a moment. The dark twinkle in his eye promised much more.

Panting, she fell on top of him and kissed his lips. "I can't get enough," she said, resting her head on top of his heart to listen to it thud in his chest.

He rubbed a hand through her tangled locks. "You never have to," he said, looking down at her.

Just then, there was a knock at the door.

Vasily looked over at it and groaned. "I'll be out in a minute, Dylan."

"It's not Dylan," Anatoly said, leaning against the entry way.

Vasily moved Lilly out of the way, slipped on his shorts and went to the door. Opening it, he looked at his boss and sighed. "What's wrong?"

Anatoly's face was impassive. "Papa wants us downstairs," he said, winking at him. "Get dressed."

"On the way," Vasily said, closing the door.

"Everything alright," Lilly asked.

"Don't know," Vasily said, putting on his clothes. "I'll be back."

***

When Vasily arrived down stairs, all three Medlov Men were waiting for him in Dmitry's study. He walked in and Boris closed the door behind him. Instantly, he felt his heart drop. The DNA test must have said something contrary to what he wanted.

Coming in, he sat down on the sofa across from them and folded his hands. Without saying a word, he waited. What bad news did they have for him? *He should have known it. A man like him didn't have happy days.   There always had to be something.*

Dmitry was sitting in his winged back leather chair with his son standing beside him. Gabriel was standing by the window with a cool gleam in his eyes. None of them were smiling.

"I've been doing a lot of thinking," Dmitry said, scratching his brow. "And after discussing it with the boys, I feel as though my decision is appropriate."

Vasily looked up from the rug. "Sir?" *What decision*, he thought to himself.

"You've grown out of your position, Vasily," Dmitry said gravely. "You have a family now." He pushed the DNA results across the desk as well as Dylan's birth certificate, signed with his own signature.

Vasily looked down at the papers and slumped his shoulders, completely confounded by the turn of events.

There was an immediate explanation. "I had the papers completed, just in case Lilly didn't make it back. We couldn't have a paternity case in court. You work for the Medlov Family for goodness sake," Dmitry huffed.

Vasily nodded. "I understand, Sir."

"The men who guard this house have one thing in common. They are without a family. They have no children. They have no wives. They don't even have steady girlfriends. They are 100% devoted to their purpose, which is to watch this family with an ever faithful eye. They cannot have vulnerabilities. They cannot have chinks in their proverbial armor. Since Lilly came into your life, your focus has changed. You have all the things that I simply cannot afford in my men." Dmitry stood up. "You can no longer be my Head of Security. Surely, you understand how it undermines the structure of this family."

Vasily concurred inwardly. He knew that his Boss was right. "I agree. My new developments put the Family at great risk, but I thank you for everything that you've done for me. I am forever grateful and eternally in your debt." He said so with such conviction that Dmitry stepped back a little.

Finally, unable to help himself, Dmitry smiled. "And that is exactly why I want you to join us, Vasily."

Anatoly cracked a smile. "It's time, brat. You've proven yourself. You need to be doing bigger things. No more standing at the watch tower, eh?"

"And we need one more on the small council, not just one more standing watch over it," Gabriel added.

Vasily looked up speechless. In all of his years, he never thought that he would ever be worthy. Sure, in the back of his mind, he had dreamt of it, but never had he imagined it coming to pass. He had no great name, no great lineage. He was just a boy from a shit part of town.

"Do you agree, brat?" Dmitry asked. "Do you think you could serve as one of my captains?"

"Yes, Sir," Vasily said, swallowing down his overwhelming emotions.

"Good," Dmitry said, walking around the table. He embraced him tight as he had never done before. "Tonight, you become one of us. It's all been arranged. The council is flying in today."

Anatoly walked over and hit Vasily on the back before he hugged him. "Did you see his face? He thought he was out of here." He laughed, but the pride couldn't help but show on his face.

Gabriel came over and offered his hand. "It will be an honor, really."

"Thank you," Vasily said, shaking Gabriel's hand for the first time ever.

"You've been like a brother to me, and now, you'll be my brother for real," Gabriel said sincerely. "Thieves-in-Law."

"Thieves-in-Law," Vasily said.

***

Leaving the men in the room to talk, Gabriel excused himself. With a purpose, he headed across the compound to Briggy's room as fast as his feet would take him. He found her there, curled up on the chaise lounge looking out of the window and sipping tea.

Closing the door behind him, he walked over and knelt before her.

"Hey," he said, moving a golden strand of hair from her face. No matter what, he couldn't deny that she was absolutely breath-taking.

"Hello," she said softly. She looked at him with red eyes.

"I'm ready for that talk," he said, sitting down on the floor beside her. His long legs stretched past the lounge chair. "And I'll stay right here until we figure it out. Phone off. Door closed. I promise." He pulled out his phone and tossed it across the room.

"Why now?" she asked, still not immune to his beauty after all this time. *How she wanted him to love her.*

Gabriel looked away. His mossy green eyes danced before he answered. "Because I'm going to the Ukraine for a while," he gave a wry smile, "and because you deserve it."

Briggy reached out and touched his face. Rubbing a hand over a freckle on his nose, she folded her knees under her. "Okay." She turned toward him completely.

"Okay," Gabriel said, looking at her stomach.

About the Author

Latrivia Nelson is proud mother of two bubbly kids, the President and CEO of RiverHouse Publishing, LLC and a senior executive for an award winning public relations firm in Memphis, TN.

When she's not running to meetings or developing strategies, she writes interracial romance and romantic suspense novels for readers across the world. With 18 titles published to date and recognized as a national bestselling author, she has something for just about anyone.

In her downtime, she loves to have a strong Jack and Coke with fiancé, Bruce Welch, watch marathon 80's movies and order take out with her family.

RIVERHOUSE
PUBLISHING

Read the Books/Buy the Books:

1. Dmitry's Closet
2. Dmitry's Royal Flush: Rise of the Queen
3. Anatoly Medlov: Complete Reign
4. Saving Anya
5. The Chronicles of Young Dmitry Medlov: Volume 1-7
6. The Ugly Girlfriend
7. Finding Opa!
8. The Grunt
9. The Contingency Plan
10. Ivy's Twisted Vine
11. The World in Reverse

www.LatriviaNelson.info